MURDER
ON
CHRISTMAS EVE

Mysteries for the Festive Season

MURDER
ON
CHRISTMAS EVE

Edited by Cecily Gayford

Ellis Peters · Julian Symons · Michael Innes
Ian Rankin · John Dickson Carr
Val McDermid · G. K. Chesterton
Marjorie Bowen · Lawrence Block
Margery Allingham

P

PROFILE BOOKS

First published in Great Britain in 2017 by
PROFILE BOOKS LTD
3 Holford Yard
Bevin Way
London WC1X 9HD
www.profilebooks.com

Selection copyright © Profile Books, 2017
See p. 234 for individual stories copyright information

3 5 7 9 10 8 6 4

Typeset in Fournier by MacGuru Ltd
Printed and bound by CPI Group (UK) Ltd, Croydon, CR0 4YY

A CIP catalogue record for this book is available from the British Library.

ISBN 978 1 78125 918 4
eISBN 978 1 78283 387 1
Book club edition ISBN 978 1 78816 021 6

Contents

The Trinity Cat

Ellis Peters

He was sitting on top of one of the rear gate-posts of the churchyard when I walked through on Christmas Eve, grooming in his lordly style, with one back leg wrapped round his neck, and his bitten ear at an angle of forty-five degrees, as usual. I reckon one of the toms he'd tangled with in his nomad days had ripped the starched bit out of that one, the other stood up sharply enough. There was snow on the ground, a thin veiling, just beginning to crackle in promise of frost before evening, but he had at least three warm refuges around the place whenever he felt like holing up, besides his two houses, which he used only for visiting and cadging.

He'd been a known character around our village for three years then, ever since he walked in from nowhere

1

and made himself agreeable to the vicar and the verger, and finding the billet comfortable and the pickings good, constituted himself resident cat to Holy Trinity church, and took over all the jobs around the place that humans were too slow to tackle, like rat-catching, and chasing off invading dogs.

Nobody knows how old he is, but I think he could only have been about two when he settled here, a scrawny, chewed-up black bandit as lean as wire. After three years of being fed by Joel Woodward at Trinity Cottage, which was the verger's house by tradition, and flanked the lych-gate on one side, and pampered and petted by Miss Patience Thomson at Church Cottage on the other side, he was double his old size, and sleek as velvet, but still had one lop ear and a kink two inches from the end of his tail. He still looked like a brigand, but a highly prosperous brigand. Nobody ever gave him a name, he wasn't the sort to get called anything fluffy or familiar. Only Miss Patience ever dared coo at him, and he was very gracious about that, she being elderly and innocent and very free with little perks like raw liver, on which he doted. One way and another, he had it made. He lived mostly outdoors, never staying in either house overnight. In winter he had his own little ground-level hatch into the furnace-room of the church, sharing his lodgings matily with a hedgehog that had qualified as assistant vermin-destructor around the churchyard, and preferred sitting out the winter among the coke to hibernating like common hedgehogs. These individualists keep turning up in our valley, for some reason.

All I'd gone to the church for that afternoon was to fix up with the vicar about the Christmas peal, having been roped into the bell-ringing team. Resident police in remote areas like ours get dragged into all sorts of activities, and when the area's changing, and new problems cropping up, if they have any sense they don't need too much dragging, but go willingly. I've put my finger on many an astonished yobbo who thought he'd got clean away with his little breaking-and-entering, just by keeping my ears open during a darts match, or choir practice.

When I came back through the churchyard, around half-past two, Miss Patience was just coming out of her gate, with a shopping bag on her wrist, and heading towards the street, and we walked along together a bit of the way. She was getting on for seventy, and hardly bigger than a bird, but very independent. Never having married or left the valley, and having looked after a mother who lived to be nearly ninety, she'd never had time to catch up with new ideas in the style of dress suitable for elderly ladies. Everything had always been done mother's way, and fashion, music, and morals had stuck at the period when mother was a carefully-brought-up girl learning domestic skills, and preparing for a chaste marriage.

There's a lot to be said for it! But it had turned Miss Patience into a frail little lady in long-skirted black or grey or navy blue, who still felt undressed without hat and gloves, at an age when Mrs Newcombe, for instance, up at the pub, favoured shocking pink trouser suits and red-gold hair-pieces. A pretty little old lady Miss Patience was, though, very straight and neat. It was a pleasure to watch her walk. Which is more than I could say for Mrs Newcombe in her trouser suit, especially from the back!

'A happy Christmas, Sergeant Moon!' she chirped at me on sight. And I wished her the same, and slowed up to her pace.

'It's going to be slippery by twilight,' I said. 'You be careful how you go.'

'Oh, I'm only going to be an hour or so,' she said serenely. 'I shall be home long before the frost sets in. I'm only doing the last bit of Christmas shopping. There's a cardigan I have to collect for Mrs Downs.' That was her cleaning-lady, who went in three mornings a week. 'I ordered it long ago, but deliveries are so slow nowadays. They've promised it for today. And a gramophone record for my little errand-boy.' Tommy Fowler that was, one of the church trebles, as pink and wholesome-looking as they usually contrive to be, and just as artful. 'And one mustn't forget our dumb friends, either, must one?' said Miss Patience cheerfully. 'They're all important, too.'

I took this to mean a couple of packets of some new product to lure wild birds to her garden. The Church Cottage thrushes were so fat they could hardly fly, and when it was frosty she put out fresh water three and four times a day.

We came to our brief street of shops, and off she went, with her big jet-and-gold brooch gleaming in her scarf. She had quite a few pieces of Victorian and Edwardian jewellery her mother'd left behind, and almost always wore one piece, being used to the belief that a lady dresses meticulously every day, not just on Sundays. And I went for a brisk walk round to see what was going on, and then went home to Molly and high tea, and took my boots off thankfully.

That was Christmas Eve. Christmas Day little Miss Thomson didn't turn up for eight o'clock Communion, which was unheard-of. The vicar said he'd call in after matins and see that she was all right, and hadn't taken cold trotting about in the snow. But somebody else beat us both to it. Tommy Fowler! He was anxious about that pop record of his. But even he had no chance until after service, for in our village it's the custom for the choir to go and sing the vicar an aubade in the shape of 'Christians, Awake!' before the main service, ignoring the fact that he's then been up four hours, and conducted two Communions. And Tommy Fowler had a solo in the anthem, too. It was a quarter-past twelve when he got away, and shot up the garden path to the door of Church Cottage.

He shot back even faster a minute later. I was heading for home when he came rocketing out of the gate and ran slam into me, with his eyes sticking out on stalks and his mouth wide open, making a sort of muted keening sound with shock. He clutched hold of me and pointed back towards Miss Thomson's front door, left half-open when he fled, and tried three times before he could croak out:

'Miss Patience ... She's there on the floor – she's bad!'

I went in on the run, thinking she'd had a heart attack all alone there, and was lying helpless. The front door led through a diminutive hall, and through another glazed door into the living-room, and that door was open, too, and there was Miss Patience face-down on the carpet, still in her coat and gloves, and with her shopping-bag lying beside her. An occasional table had been knocked over in her fall, spilling a vase and a book. Her hat was askew over one ear, and caved in like a trodden mushroom, and her neat grey bun of hair had come undone and trailed on her shoulder, and it was no longer grey but soiled, brownish black. She was dead and stiff. The room was so cold, you could tell those doors had been ajar all night.

The kid had followed me in, hanging on to my sleeve, his teeth chattering. 'I didn't open the door – it was open!

I didn't touch her, or anything. I only came to see if she was all right, and get my record.'

It was there, lying unbroken, half out of the shopping-bag by her arm. She'd meant it for him, and I told him he should have it, but not yet, because it might be evidence, and we mustn't move anything. And I got him out of there quick, and gave him to the vicar to cope with, and went back to Miss Patience as soon as I'd telephoned for the outfit. Because we had a murder on our hands.

So that was the end of one gentle, harmless old woman, one of very many these days, battered to death because she walked in on an intruder who panicked. Walked in on him, I judged, not much more than an hour after I left her in the street. Everything about her looked the same as then, the shopping-bag, the coat, the hat, the gloves. The only difference, that she was dead. No, one more thing! No handbag, unless it was under the body, and later, when we were able to move her, I wasn't surprised to see that it wasn't there. Handbags are where old ladies carry their money. The sneak-thief who panicked and lashed out at her had still had greed and presence of mind enough to grab the bag as he fled. Nobody'd have to describe that bag to me, I knew it well, soft black leather with an old-fashioned gilt clasp and a short handle, a small thing, not like the holdalls they carry nowadays.

She was lying facing the opposite door, also open, which

led to the stairs. On the writing-desk by that door stood one of a pair of heavy brass candlesticks. Its fellow was on the floor, beside Miss Thomson's body, and though the bun of hair and the felt hat had prevented any great spattering of blood, there was blood enough on the square base to label the weapon. Whoever had hit her had been just sneaking down the stairs, ready to leave. She'd come home barely five minutes too soon.

Upstairs, in her bedroom, her bits of jewellery hadn't taken much finding. She'd never thought of herself as having valuables, or of other people as coveting them. Her gold and turquoise and funereal jet and true-lover's-knots in gold and opals, and mother's engagement and wedding rings, and her little Edwardian pendant watch set with seed pearls, had simply lived in the small top drawer of her dressing-table. She belonged to an honest epoch, and it was gone, and now she was gone after it. She didn't even lock her door when she went shopping. There wouldn't have been so much as the warning of a key grating in the lock, just the door opening.

Ten years ago not a soul in this valley behaved differently from Miss Patience. Nobody locked doors, sometimes not even overnight. Some of us went on a fortnight's holiday and left the doors unlocked. Now we can't even put out the milk money until the milkman knocks at the door in person. If this generation likes to pride itself on its progress, let it! As for me, I thought suddenly that maybe the innocent was well out of it.

We did the usual things, photographed the body and the scene of the crime, the doctor examined her and authorised her removal, and confirmed what I'd supposed about the approximate time of her death. And the forensic boys lifted a lot of smudgy latents that weren't going to be of any use to anybody, because they weren't going to be on record, barring a million to one chance. The whole thing stank of the amateur. There wouldn't be any easy matching up of prints, even if they got beauties. One more thing we did for Miss Patience. We tolled the dead-bell for her on Christmas night, six heavy, muffled strokes. She was a virgin. Nobody had to vouch for it, we all knew. And let me point out, it is a title of honour, to be respected accordingly.

We'd hardly got the poor soul out of the house when the Trinity cat strolled in, taking advantage of the minute or two while the door was open. He got as far as the place on the carpet where she'd lain, and his fur and whiskers stood on end, and even his lop ear jerked up straight. He put his nose down to the pile of the Wilton, about where her shopping bag and handbag must have lain, and started going round in interested circles, snuffing the floor and making little throaty noises that might have been distress, but sounded like pleasure. Excitement,

9

anyhow. The chaps from the CID were still busy, and didn't want him under their feet, so I picked him up and took him with me when I went across to Trinity Cottage to talk to the verger.

The cat never liked being picked up, after a minute he started clawing and cursing, and I put him down. He stalked away again at once, past the corner where people shot their dead flowers, out at the lych-gate, and straight back to sit on Miss Thomson's doorstep. Well, after all, he used to get fed there, he might well be uneasy at all these queer comings and goings. And they don't say 'as curious as a cat' for nothing, either.

I didn't need telling that Joel Woodward had had no hand in what had happened, he'd been nearest neighbour and good friend to Miss Patience for years, but he might have seen or heard something out of the ordinary. He was a little, wiry fellow, gnarled like a tree-root, the kind that goes on spry and active into his nineties, and then decides that's enough, and leaves overnight. His wife was dead long ago, and his daughter had come back to keep house for him after her husband deserted her, until she died, too, in a bus accident. There was just old Joel now, and the grandson she'd left with him, young Joel Barnett, nineteen, and a bit of a tearaway by his grandad's standards, but so far pretty innocuous by mine. He was a sulky, graceless sort, but he did work, and he stuck with the old man when many another would have lit out elsewhere.

'A bad business,' said old Joel, shaking his head. 'I only wish I could help you lay hands on whoever did it. But I only saw her yesterday morning about ten, when she took in the milk. I was round at the church hall all afternoon, getting things ready for the youth social they had last night, it was dark before I got back. I never saw or heard anything out of place. You can't see her living-room light from here, so there was no call to wonder. But the lad was here all afternoon. They only work till one, Christmas Eve. Then they all went boozing together for an hour or so, I expect, so I don't know exactly what time he got in, but he was here and had the tea on when I came home. Drop round in an hour or so and he should be here, he's gone round to collect this girl he's mashing. There's a party somewhere tonight.'

I dropped round accordingly, and young Joel was there, sure enough, shoulder-length hair, frilled shirt, outsize lapels and all, got up to kill, all for the benefit of the girl his grandad had mentioned. And it turned out to be Connie Dymond, from the comparatively respectable branch of the family, along the canal-side. There were three sets of Dymond cousins, boys, no great harm in 'em but worth watching, but only this one girl in Connie's family. A good-looker, or at least most of the lads seemed to think so, she had a dozen or so on her string before she took up with young Joel. Big girl, too, with a lot of mauve eye-shadow and a mother-of-pearl mouth, in huge platform shoes and the fashionable drab granny-coat. But she was acting very prim and proper with old Joel around.

'Half-past two when I got home,' said young Joel. 'Grandad was round at the hall, and I'd have gone round to help him, only I'd had a pint or two, and after I'd had me dinner I went to sleep, so it wasn't worth it by the time I woke up. Around four, that'd be. From then on I was here watching the telly, and I never saw nor heard a thing. But there was nobody else here, so I could be spinning you the yarn, if you want to look at it that way.'

He had a way of going looking for trouble before anybody else suggested it, there was nothing new about that. Still, there it was. One young fellow on the spot, and minus any alibi. There'd be plenty of others in the same case.

In the evening he'd been at the church social. Miss Patience wouldn't be expected there, it was mainly for the young, and anyhow, she very seldom went out in the evenings.

'*I* was there with Joel,' said Connie Dymond. 'He called for me at seven, I was with him all the evening. We went home to our place after the social finished, and he didn't leave till nearly midnight.'

Very firm about it she was, doing her best for him. She could hardly know that his movements in the evening didn't interest us, since Miss Patience had then been dead for some hours.

When I opened the door to leave, the Trinity cat walked in, stalking past me with a purposeful stride. He had a look round us all, and then made for the girl, reached up his front paws to her knees, and was on her lap before she could fend him off, though she didn't look as if she welcomed his attentions. Very civil he was, purring and rubbing himself against her coat sleeve, and poking his whiskery face into hers. Unusual for him to be effusive, but when he did decide on it, it was always with someone who couldn't stand cats. You'll have noticed it's a way they have.

'Shove him off,' said young Joel, seeing she didn't at all care for being singled out. 'He only does it to annoy people.'

And she did, but he only jumped on again, I noticed as I closed the door on them and left. It was a Dymond party they were going to, the senior lot, up at the filling station. Not much point in trying to check up on all her cousins and swains when they were gathered for a booze-up. Coming out of a hangover, tomorrow, they might be easy meat. Not that I had any special reason to look their way, they were an extrovert lot, more given to grievous bodily harm in street punch-ups than anything secretive. But it was wide open.

Well, we summed up. None of the lifted prints was on record, all we could do in that line was exclude all those that were Miss Thomson's. This kind of sordid little opportunist break-in had come into local experience only fairly recently, and though it was no novelty now, it had never before led to a death. No motive but the impulse of greed, so no traces leading up to the act, and none leading away. Everyone connected with the church, and most of the village besides, knew about the bits of jewellery she had, but never before had anyone considered them as desirable loot. Victoriana now carry inflated values, and are in demand, but this still didn't look calculated, just wanton. A kid's crime, a teenager's crime. Or the crime of a permanent teenager. They start at twelve years old now, but there are also the shiftless louts who never get beyond twelve years old, even in their forties.

We checked all the obvious people, her part-time gardener – but he was demonstrably elsewhere at the time – and his drifter of a son, whose alibi was non-existent but voluble, the window-cleaner, a sidelong soul who played up his ailments and did rather well out of her, all the delivery men. Several there who were clear, one or two who could have been around, but had no particular reason to be.

Then we went after all the youngsters who, on their records, were possibles. There were three with breaking-and-entering convictions, but if they'd been there they'd been gloved. Several others with petty theft against them were also without alibis. By the end of a pretty exhaustive survey the field was wide, and none of the runners seemed to be ahead of the rest, and we were still looking. None of the stolen property had so far showed up.

Not, that is, until the Saturday. I was coming from Church Cottage through the graveyard again, and as I came near the corner where the dead flowers were shot, I noticed a glaring black patch making an irregular hole in the veil of frozen snow that still covered the ground. You couldn't miss it, it showed up like a black eye. And part of it was the soil and rotting leaves showing through, and part, the blackest part, was the Trinity cat, head down and back arched, digging industriously like a terrier after a rat. The bent end of his tail lashed steadily, while the remaining eight inches stood erect.

If he knew I was standing watching him, he didn't care. Nothing was going to deflect him from what he was doing. And in a minute or two he heaved his prize clear, and clawed out to the light a little black leather handbag with a gilt clasp. No mistaking it, all stuck over as it was with dirt and rotting leaves. And he loved it, he was patting it and playing with it and rubbing his head against it, and purring like a steam-engine. He cursed, though, when I took it off him, and walked round and round me, pawing and swearing, telling me and the world he'd found it, and it was his.

It hadn't been there long. I'd been along that path often enough to know that the snow hadn't been disturbed the day before. Also, the mess of humus fell off it pretty quick and clean, and left it hardly stained at all. I held it in my handkerchief and snapped the catch, and the inside was clean and empty, the lining slightly frayed from long use. The Trinity cat stood upright on his hind legs and protested loudly, and he had a voice that could outshout a Siamese.

Somebody behind me said curiously: 'Whatever've you got there?' And there was young Joel standing open-mouthed, staring, with Connie Dymond hanging on to his arm and gaping at the cat's find in horrified recognition.

'Oh, no! My gawd, that's Miss Thomson's bag, isn't it? I've seen her carrying it hundreds of times.'

'Did *he* dig it up?' said Joel, incredulous. 'You reckon the chap who – you know, *him!* – he buried it there? It could be anybody, everybody uses this way through.'

'My gawd!' said Connie, shrinking in fascinated horror against his side. 'Look at that cat! You'd think he *knows* ... He gives me the shivers! What's got into him?'

What, indeed? After I'd got rid of them and taken the bag away with me I was still wondering. I walked away with his prize and he followed me as far as the road, howling and swearing, and once I put the bag down, open, to see what he'd do, and he pounced on it and started his fun and games again until I took it from him. For the life of me I couldn't see what there was about it to delight him, but he was in no doubt. I was beginning to feel right superstitious about this avenging detective cat, and to wonder what he was going to unearth next.

I know I ought to have delivered the bag to the forensic lab, but somehow I hung on to it overnight. There was something fermenting at the back of my mind that I couldn't yet grasp.

Next morning we had two more at morning service besides the regulars. Young Joel hardly ever went to church, and I doubt if anybody'd ever seen Connie Dymond there before, but there they both were, large as life and solemn as death, in a middle pew, the boy sulky and scowling as if he'd been press-ganged into it, as he certainly had, Connie very subdued and big-eyed, with almost no make-up and an unusually grave and thoughtful face. Sudden death brings people up against daunting possibilities, and creates penitents. Young Joel felt silly there, but he was daft about her, plainly enough, she could get him to do what she wanted, and she'd wanted to make this gesture. She went through all the movements of devotion, he just sat, stood and kneeled awkwardly as required, and went on scowling.

There was a bitter east wind when we came out. On the steps of the porch everybody dug out gloves and turned up collars against it, and so did young Joel, and as he hauled his gloves out of his coat pocket, out with them came a little bright thing that rolled down the steps in front of us all and came to rest in a crack between the flagstones of the path. A gleam of pale blue and gold. A dozen people must have recognised it. Mrs Downs gave tongue in a shriek that informed even those who hadn't.

'That's Miss Thomson's! It's one of her turquoise earrings! *How did you get hold of that, Joel Barnett?*'

How, indeed? Everybody stood staring at the tiny thing, and then at young Joel, and he was gazing at the flagstones, struck white and dumb. And all in a moment Connie Dymond had pulled her arm free of his and recoiled from him until her back was against the wall, and was edging away from him like somebody trying to get out of range of flood or fire, and her face a sight to be seen, blind and stiff with horror.

'You!' she said in a whisper. 'It was you! Oh, my God, *you* did it – *you* killed her! And me keeping company – how could I? How could *you!*'

She let out a screech and burst into sobs, and before anybody could stop her she turned and took to her heels, running for home like a mad thing.

I let her go. She'd keep. And I got young Joel and that

single ear-ring away from the Sunday congregation and into Trinity Cottage before half the people there knew what was happening, and shut the world out, all but old Joel who came panting and shaking after us a few minutes later.

The boy was a long time getting his voice back, and when he did he had nothing to say but, hopelessly, over and over: 'I didn't! I never touched her, I wouldn't. I don't know how that thing got into my pocket. I didn't do it. I never …'

Human beings are not all that inventive. Given a similar set of circumstances they tend to come out with the same formula. And in any case, 'deny everything and say nothing else' is a very good rule when cornered.

They thought I'd gone round the bend when I said: 'Where's the cat? See if you can get him in.'

Old Joel was past wondering. He went out and rattled a saucer on the steps, and pretty soon the Trinity cat strolled in. Not at all excited, not wanting anything, fed and lazy, just curious enough to come and see why he was wanted. I turned him loose on young Joel's overcoat, and he couldn't have cared less. The pocket that had held the ear-ring held very little interest for him. He didn't care about any of the clothes in the wardrobe, or on the pegs in the little hall. As far as he was concerned, this new find was a non-event.

I sent for a constable and a car, and took young Joel in with me to the station, and all the village, you may be sure, either saw us pass or heard about it very shortly after. But I didn't stop to take any statement from him, just left him there, and took the car up to Mary Melton's place, where she breeds Siamese, and borrowed a cat-basket from her, the sort she uses to carry her queens to the vet. She asked what on earth I wanted it for, and I said to take the Trinity cat for a ride. She laughed her head off.

'Well, *he's* no queen,' she said, 'and no king, either. Not even a jack! And you'll never get that wild thing into a basket.'

'Oh, yes, I will,' I said. 'And if he isn't any of the other picture cards, he's probably going to turn out to be the joker.'

A very neat basket it was, not too obviously meant for a cat. And it was no trick getting the Trinity cat into it, all I did was drop in Miss Thomson's handbag, and he was in after it in a moment. He growled when he found himself shut in, but it was too late to complain then.

At the house by the canal Connie Dymond's mother let me in, but was none too happy about letting me see Connie, until I explained that I needed a statement from her before I could fit together young Joel's movements all through those Christmas days.

Naturally I understood that the girl was terribly upset,

but she'd had a lucky escape, and the sooner everything was cleared up, the better for her. And it wouldn't take long.

It didn't take long. Connie came down the stairs readily enough when her mother called her. She was all stained and pale and tearful, but had perked up somewhat with a sort of shivering pride in her own prominence. I've seen them like that before, getting the juice out of being the centre of attention even while they wish they were else-where. You could even say she hurried down, and she left the door of her bedroom open behind her, by the light coming through at the head of the stairs.

'Oh, Sergeant Moon!' she quavered at me from three steps up. 'Isn't it *awful*? I still can't believe it! *Can* there be some mistake? Is there any chance it *wasn't*...?'

I said soothingly, yes, there was always a chance. And I slipped the latch of the cat-basket with one hand, so that the flap fell open, and the Trinity cat was out of there and up those stairs like a black flash, startling her so much she nearly fell down the last step, and steadied herself against the wall with a small shriek. And I blurted apologies for accidentally loosing him, and went up the stairs three at a time ahead of her, before she could recover her balance.

He was up on his hind legs in her dolly little room, full of pop posters and frills and garish colours, pawing at the second drawer of her dressing-table, and singing a loud,

21

joyous, impatient song. When I came plunging in, he even looked over his shoulder at me and stood down, as though he knew I'd open the drawer for him. And I did, and he was up among her fancy undies like a shot, and digging with his front paws.

He found what he wanted just as she came in at the door. He yanked it out from among her bras and slips, and tossed it into the air, and in seconds he was on the floor with it, rolling and wrestling it, juggling it on his four paws like a circus turn, and purring fit to kill, a cat in ecstasy. A comic little thing it was, a muslin mouse with a plaited green nylon string for a tail, yellow beads for eyes, and nylon threads for whiskers, that rustled and sent out wafts of strong scent as he batted it around and sang to it. A catmint mouse, old Miss Thomson's last-minute purchase from the pet shop for her dumb friend. If you could ever call the Trinity cat dumb! The only thing she bought that day small enough to be slipped into her handbag instead of the shopping bag.

Connie let out a screech, and was across that room so fast I only just beat her to the open drawer. They were all there, the little pendant watch, the locket, the brooches, the true-lover's-knot, the purse, even the other ear-ring. A mistake, she should have ditched both while she was about it, but she was too greedy. They were for pierced ears, anyhow, no good to Connie.

I held them out in the palm of my hand – such a large haul they made – and let her see what she'd robbed and killed for.

If she'd kept her head she might have made a fight of it even then, claimed he'd made her hide them for him, and she'd been afraid to tell on him directly, and could only think of staging that public act at church, to get him safely in custody before she came clean. But she went wild. She did the one deadly thing, turned and kicked out in a screaming fury at the Trinity cat. He was spinning like a humming-top, and all she touched was the kink in his tail. He whipped round and clawed a red streak down her leg through the nylon. And then she screamed again, and began to babble through hysterical sobs that she never meant to hurt the poor old sod, that it wasn't her fault! Ever since she'd been going with young Joel she'd been seeing that little old bag going in and out, draped with her bits of gold. What in hell did an old witch like her want with jewellery? She had no *right*! At her age!

'But I never meant to hurt her! She came in too soon,' lamented Connie, still and for ever the aggrieved. 'What was I supposed to do? I had to get away, didn't I? *She was between me and the door!*'

She was half her size, too, and nearly four times her age! Ah well! What the courts would do with Connie, thank God, was none of my business. I just took her in and charged her, and got her statement. Once we had her dabs it was all over, because she'd left a bunch of them sweaty and clear on that brass candlestick. But if it hadn't been for the Trinity cat and his single-minded pursuit, scaring her into that ill-judged attempt to hand us young Joel as a scapegoat, she might, she just might, have got clean away with it. At least the boy could go home now, and count his blessings.

Not that she was very bright, of course. Who but a stupid harpy, soaked in cheap perfume and gimcrack dreams, would have hung on even to the catmint mouse, mistaking it for an herbal sachet to put among her smalls?

I saw the Trinity cat only this morning, sitting grooming in the church porch. He's getting very self-important, as if he knows he's a celebrity, though throughout he was only looking after the interests of Number One, like all cats. He's lost interest in his mouse already, now most of the scent's gone.

The Santa Claus Club

Julian Symons

It is not often, in real life, that letters are written recording implacable hatred nursed over the years, or that private detectives are invited by peers to select dining clubs, or that murders occur at such dining clubs, or that they are solved on the spot by a process of deduction. The case of the Santa Claus Club provided an example of all these rarities.

The case began one day, a week before Christmas, when Francis Quarles went to see Lord Acrise. He was a rich man, Lord Acrise, and an important one, the chairman of this big building concern and director of that and the other insurance company, and consultant to the Government on half a dozen matters. He had been a harsh, intolerant man in his prime, and was still hard enough in his early seventies, Quarles guessed, as he looked at the beaky nose, jutting chin, and stony blue eyes.

They sat in the study of Acrise's house just off the Brompton Road.

'Just tell me what you think of these,' Lord Acrise said.

These were three letters, badly typed on a machine with a worn ribbon. They were all signed with the name James Gliddon. The first two contained vague references to some wrong done to Gliddon by Acrise in the past. They were written in language that was wild but unmistakably threatening. *You have been a whited sepulchre for too long, but now your time has come ... You don't know what I'm going to do, now I've come back, but you won't be able to help wondering and worrying ... The mills of God grind slowly, but they're going to grind you into little bits for what you've done to me.*

The third letter was more specific. *So the thief is going to play Santa Claus. That will be your last evening alive. I shall be there, Joe Acrise, and I shall watch with pleasure as you squirm in agony.*

Quarles looked at the envelopes. They were plain and cheap. The address was typed, and the word *Personal* was on top of each envelope. 'Who is James Gliddon?' he asked.

The stony eyes glared at him. 'I'm told you're to be trusted. Gliddon was a school friend of mine. We grew up together in the slums of Nottingham. We started a building company together. It did well for a time, then went bust. There was a lot of money missing. Gliddon kept the books. He got five years for fraud.'

'Have you heard from him since then? I see all these letters are recent.'

'He's written half a dozen letters, I suppose, over the years. The last one came – oh, seven years ago, I should think. From the Argentine.' Acrise stopped, then added abruptly, 'Snewin tried to find him for me, but he'd disappeared.'

'Snewin?'

'My secretary. Been with me twelve years.'

He pressed a bell. An obsequious, fattish man, whose appearance somehow put Quarles in mind of an enormous mouse, scurried in.

'Snewin – did we keep any of those old letters from Gliddon?'

'No sir. You told me to destroy them.'

'The last ones came from the Argentine, right?'

'From Buenos Aires, to be exact, sir.'

Acrise nodded, and Snewin scurried out.

Quarles said, 'Who else knows this story about Gliddon?'

'Just my wife.'

'And what does this mean about you playing Santa

27

Claus?' 'I'm this year's chairman of the Santa Claus Club. We hold our raffle and dinner next Monday.' Then Quarles remembered. The Santa Claus Club had been formed by ten rich men. Each year they met, every one of them dressed up as Santa Claus, and held a raffle. The members took it in turn to provide the prize that was raffled – it might be a case of Napoleon brandy, a modest cottage with some exclusive salmon fishing rights attached to it, or a Constable painting. Each Santa Claus bought one ticket for the raffle, at a cost of one thousand guineas. The total of ten thousand guineas was given to a Christmas charity. After the raffle the assembled Santa Clauses, each accompanied by one guest, ate a traditional English Christmas dinner.

The whole thing was a combination of various English characteristics: enjoyment of dressing up, a wish to help charities, and the desire also that the help given should not go unrecorded.

'I want you to find Gliddon,' Lord Acrise said. 'Don't mistake me, Mr Quarles. I don't want to take action against him, I want to help him. I wasn't to blame, don't think I admit that, but it was hard that Jimmy Gliddon should go to jail. I'm a hard man, have been all my life, but I don't think my worst enemies would call me mean. Those who've helped me know that when I die they'll find they're not forgotten. Jimmy Gliddon must be an old man now. I'd like to set him up for the rest of his life.'

'To find him by next Monday is a tall order,' Quarles said. 'But I'll try.' He was at the door when Acrise said, 'By the way, I'd like you to be my guest at the Club dinner on Monday night …'

There were two ways of trying to find Gliddon: by investigation of his career after leaving prison, and through the typewritten letters. Quarles took the job of tracing the past, leaving the letters to his secretary, Molly Player.

From Scotland Yard he found out that Gliddon had spent nearly four years in prison, from 1913 to late 1916. He had joined a Nottinghamshire regiment when he came out, and the records of this regiment showed that he had been demobilised in August, 1919, with the rank of Sergeant. In 1923 he had been given a sentence of three years for an attempt to smuggle diamonds. Thereafter all trace of him in Britain vanished.

Quarles made some expensive telephone calls to Buenos Aires, where the letters had come from seven years earlier. He learned that Gliddon had lived in that city from a time just after the Second World War until 1955. He ran an import-export business, and was thought to have been living in other South American Republics during the war. His business was said to have been a cloak for smuggling, both of drugs and of suspected Nazis, whom he got out of Europe into the Argentine. In 1955 a newspaper had accused Gliddon of arranging the entry into the Argentine of a Nazi war criminal named Hermann Breit. Gliddon disappeared. A couple of weeks later a battered body was washed up just outside the city.

'It was identified as Señor Gliddon,' the liquid voice said over the telephone. 'But you know, Señor Quarles, in such matters the police are sometimes unhappy to close their files.'

'There was still some doubt?'

'Yes. Not very much, perhaps. But in these cases there is often a measure of doubt.'

Molly Player found out nothing useful about the paper and envelopes. They were of the sort that could be bought in a thousand stores and shops in London and elsewhere. She had no more luck with the typewriter.

Lord Acrise made no comment on Quarles's recital of failure. 'See you on Monday evening, seven-thirty, black tie,' he said, and barked with laughter. 'Your host will be Santa Claus.'

'I'd like to be there earlier.'

'Good idea. Any time you like. You know where it is? Robert the Devil Restaurant ...'

The Robert the Devil Restaurant is situated inconspicuously in Mayfair. It is not a restaurant in the ordinary sense of the word, for there is no public dining-room, but simply several private rooms accommodating any number of guests from two to thirty. Perhaps the food is not quite the best in London, but it is certainly the most expensive.

It was here that Quarles arrived at half-past six, a big, suave man, rather too conspicuously elegant perhaps in a midnight-blue dinner jacket. He talked to Albert, the *maitre d'hotel,* whom he had known for some years, took an unobtrusive look at the waiters, went into and admired the sparkling kitchens. Albert observed his activities with tolerant amusement. 'You are here on some sort of business, Mr Quarles?'

'I am a guest, Albert. I am also a kind of bodyguard. Tell me, how many of your waiters have joined you in the past twelve months?'

'Perhaps half a dozen. They come, they go.'

'Is there anybody at all on your staff – waiters, kitchen staff, anybody – who has joined you in the past year, and who is over sixty years old?'

'No. There is not such a one.'

The first of the guests came just after a quarter-past seven. This was the brain surgeon Sir James Erdington, with a guest whom Quarles recognized as the Arctic explorer, Norman Endell. After that they came at intervals of a minute or two: a junior minister in the Government; one of the three most important men in the motor industry; a general elevated to the peerage to celebrate his retirement; a theatrical producer named Roddy Davis, who had successfully combined commerce and culture.

As they arrived, the hosts went into a special robing room to put on their Santa Claus clothes, while the guests drank sherry.

At seven-twenty-five Snewin scurried in, gasped, 'Excuse me, place names, got to put them out,' and went into the dining-room. Through the open door Quarles glimpsed a large oval table, gleaming with silver, bright with roses.

After Snewin came Lord Acrise, jutting-nosed and fearsome-eyed. 'Sorry to have kept you waiting,' he barked, and asked conspiratorially, 'Well?'

'No sign.'

'False alarm. Lot of nonsense. Got to dress up now.'

He went into the robing room with his box – each of the hosts had a similar box, labelled 'Santa Claus' – and came out again bewigged, bearded, and robed. 'Better get the business over, and then we can enjoy ourselves. You can tell 'em to come in,' he said to Albert.

This referred to the photographers, who had been clustered outside, and now came into the room specially provided for holding the raffle. In the centre of the room was a table, and on the table stood this year's prize, two exquisite T'ang horses. On the other side of the table were ten chairs arranged in a semicircle, and on these sat the Santa Clauses. Their guests stood inconspicuously at the side.

The raffle was conducted with the utmost seriousness. Each Santa Claus had a numbered slip. These slips were put into a tombola, and Acrise put in his hand and drew out one of them. Flash bulbs exploded.

'The number drawn is eight,' Acrise announced, and Roddy Davis waved the counterfoil in his hand.

'Isn't that *wonderful*? It's my ticket.' He went over to the horses, picked up one. 'I'm bound to say that they couldn't have gone to *anybody* who'd have appreciated them more.'

Quarles, standing near the general, whose face was as red as his robe, heard him mutter something uncomplimentary. Charity, he reflected, was not universal, even in a gathering of Santa Clauses. Then there were more flashes, the photographers disappeared, and Quarles's views about the nature of charity were reinforced when, as they were about to go into the dining-room, Sir James Erdington said, 'Forgotten something, haven't you, Acrise?'

With what seemed dangerous quietness Acrise answered, 'Have I? I don't think so.'

'It's customary for the Club and guests to sing "Noel" before we go in to dinner.'

'You didn't come to last year's dinner. It was agreed

33

then that we should give it up. Carols after dinner, much better.'

'I must say I thought that was just for last year, because we were late,' Roddy Davis fluted.

'Suggest we put it to the vote,' Erdington said sharply.

Half a dozen of the Santas now stood looking at each other with subdued hostility. Then suddenly the Arctic explorer, Endell, began to sing 'Noel, Noel' in a rich bass. There was the faintest flicker of hesitation, and then the guests and their hosts joined in. The situation was saved.

At dinner Quarles found himself with Acrise on one side of him and Roddy Davis on the other. Endell sat at Acrise's other side, and beyond him was Erdington. Turtle soup was followed by grilled sole, and then three great turkeys were brought in. The helpings of turkey were enormous. With the soup they drank a light, dry sherry, with the sole Chassagne Montrachet, with the turkey an Aloxe Corton.

'And who are *you*?' Roddy Davis peered at Quarles's card and said, 'Of course, I know your name.'

'I am a criminologist.' This sounded better, Quarles thought, than 'private detective'.

'I remember your monograph on criminal calligraphy. Quite fascinating.'

So Davis *did* know who he was. It would be easy, Quarles thought, to underrate the intelligence of this man.

'These beards really do get in the way rather,' Davis said. 'But there, one must suffer for tradition. Have you known Acrise long?'

'Not very. I'm greatly privileged to be here.'

Quarles had been watching, as closely as he could, the pouring of the wine, the serving of the food. He had seen nothing suspicious. Now, to get away from Davis's questions, he turned to his host.

'Damned awkward business before dinner,' Acrise said. 'Might have been, at least. Can't let well alone, Erdington.'

He picked up his turkey leg, attacked it with Elizabethan gusto, wiped his mouth and fingers with his napkin. 'Like this wine?'

'It's excellent.'

'Chose it myself. They've got some good Burgundies here.' Acrise's speech was slightly slurred, and it seemed to Quarles that he was rapidly getting drunk.

'Do you have any speeches?'

'No speeches. Just sing carols. But I've got a little surprise for 'em.'

'What sort of surprise?'

'Very much in the spirit of Christmas, and a good joke too. But if I told you, it wouldn't be a surprise, would it?'

There was a general cry of pleasure as Albert himself brought in the great plum pudding, topped with holly and blazing with brandy.

'That's the most wonderful pudding I've ever seen in my life,' Endell said. 'Are we really going to eat it?'

'Of course,' Acrise said irritably. He stood up, swaying a little, and picked up the knife beside the pudding.

'I don't like to be critical, but our Chairman is really not cutting the pudding very well,' Roddy Davis whispered to Quarles. And indeed, it was more of a stab than a cut that Acrise made at the pudding. Albert took over, and cut it quickly and efficiently. Bowls of brandy butter were circulated.

Quarles leaned towards Acrise. 'Are you all right?'

'Of course I'm all right.'

The slurring was very noticeable now. Acrise ate no pudding, but he drank some more wine, and dabbed at his lips. When the pudding was finished, he got slowly to his feet again and toasted the Queen. Cigars were lighted. Acrise was not smoking. He whispered something to the waiter, who nodded and left the room. Acrise got up again, leaning heavily on the table.

'A little surprise,' he said. 'In the spirit of Christmas.'

Quarles had thought that he was beyond being surprised by the activities of the Santa Claus Club, but he was astonished at the sight of the three figures who entered the room.

They were led by Snewin, somehow more mouselike than ever, wearing a long, white smock and a red nightcap with a tassel. He was followed by an older man dressed in a kind of grey sackcloth, with a face so white that it might have been covered in plaster of Paris. This man carried chains, which he shook. At the rear came a young-middle-aged lady who seemed to be completely hung with tinsel.

'I am Scrooge,' said Snewin.

'I am Marley,' wailed grey sackcloth, clanking his chains vigorously.

'And I,' said the young-middle-aged lady, with abominable sprightliness, 'am the ghost of Christmas past.'

There was a ripple of laughter.

'We have come,' said Snewin in a thin, mouse voice, 'to perform for you our own interpretation of *A Christmas Carol* ... Oh, sir, what's the matter?'

Lord Acrise stood up in his robes, tore off his wig, pulled at his beard, tried to say something. Then he clutched at the side of his chair and fell sideways, so that he leaned heavily against Endell and slipped slowly to the floor.

There ensued a minute of confused, important activity. Endell made some sort of exclamation and rose from his chair, slightly obstructing Quarles. Erdington was first beside the body, holding the wrist in his hand, listening for the heart. Then they were all crowding round. Snewin, at Quarles's left shoulder, was babbling something, and at his right were Roddy Davis and Endell.

'Stand back,' Erdington snapped. He stayed on his knees for another few moments, looking curiously at Acrise's puffed, distorted face, bluish around the mouth. Then he stood up.

'He's dead.'

There was a murmur of surprise and horror, and now they all drew back, as men do instinctively from the presence of death. 'Heart attack?' somebody said.

Quarles moved to his side. 'I'm a private detective, Sir James. Lord Acrise feared an attempt on his life, and asked me to come along here.'

'You seem to have done well so far,' Erdington said drily. 'May I look at the body?'

'If you wish.'

As Quarles bent down, he caught the smell of bitter almonds. 'There's a smell like prussic acid, but the way he died precludes cyanide, I think. He seemed to become very drunk during dinner, and his speech was slurred. Does that suggest anything to you?'

'I'm a brain surgeon, not a physician.' Erdington stared at the floor. 'Nitro benzene?'

'That's what I thought. We shall have to notify the police.'

Quarles went to the door and spoke to a disturbed Albert. Then he returned to the room and clapped his hands.

'Gentlemen. My name is Francis Quarles, and I am a private detective. Lord Acrise asked me to come here tonight because he had received a threat that this would be his last evening alive. The threat said, "I shall be there, and I shall watch with pleasure as you squirm in agony." Lord Acrise has been poisoned. It seems certain that the man who made the threat is in this room.'

'Gliddon,' a voice said. Snewin had divested himself of the white smock and red nightcap, and now appeared as his customary respectable self.

'Yes. This letter, and others he had received, were signed with the name of James Gliddon, a man who bore a grudge against Lord Acrise which went back nearly half a century. Gliddon became a professional smuggler and crook. He would now be in his late sixties.'

'But dammit, man, this Gliddon's not here.' That was the General, who took off his wig and beard. 'Lot of tomfoolery.'

In a shamefaced way the other members of the Santa Claus Club removed their facial trappings. Marley took off his chains and the lady discarded her cloak of tinsel.

Quarles said, 'Isn't he here? But Lord Acrise is dead.' Snewin coughed. 'Excuse me, sir, but would it be possible for my colleagues from our local dramatic society to retire?'

'Everybody must stay in this room until the police

arrive,' Quarles said grimly. 'The problem, as you will all realize, is how the poison was administered. All of us ate the same food, drank the same wine. I sat next to Lord Acrise, and I watched as closely as possible to make sure of this. After dinner some of you smoked cigars or cigarettes, but not Lord Acrise.'

'Just a moment.' It was Roddy Davis who spoke. 'This sounds fantastic, but wasn't it Sherlock Holmes who said that when you'd eliminated all other possibilities, even a fantastic one must be right? Supposing poison in powder form was put on to Acrise's food? Through the pepper pots, say …'

Erdington was shaking his head, but Quarles unscrewed both salt and pepper pots and tasted their contents. 'Salt and pepper,' he said briefly. 'Hello, what's this?'

'It's Acrise's napkin,' Endell said. 'What's remarkable about that?'

'It's a napkin, but not the one Acrise used. He wiped his mouth half a dozen times on his napkin, and wiped his greasy fingers on it too, when he'd gnawed a turkey bone. He must certainly have left grease marks on it. But look at this napkin.'

He held it up, and they saw that it was spotless. Quarles said softly, 'The murderer's mistake.'

Quarles turned to Erdington. 'Sir James and I agree that the poison used was probably nitro benzene. This is deadly as a liquid, but it is also poisonous as a vapour – isn't that so?'

Erdington nodded. 'You'll remember the case of the unfortunate young man who used shoe polish containing nitro benzene on damp shoes, put them on and wore them, and was killed by the fumes.'

'Yes. Somebody made sure that Lord Acrise had a napkin that had been soaked in nitro benzene but was dry enough to use. The same person substituted the proper napkin, the one belonging to the restaurant, after Acrise was dead.'

'That means the napkin must still be here,' Davis said. 'It does.'

'Then I vote that we submit to a search!'

'That won't be necessary,' Quarles said. 'Only one person here fulfils all the qualifications of the murderer.'

'James Gliddon?'

'No. Gliddon is almost certainly dead, as I found out when I made enquiries about him. But the murderer is somebody who knew about Acrise's relationship with Gliddon, and tried to be clever by writing those letters to lead us along a wrong track.' He paused. 'Then the murderer is somebody who had the opportunity of coming in here before dinner, and who knew exactly where Acrise would be sitting.'

There was a dead silence in the room.

Quarles said, 'He removed any possible suspicion from himself, as he thought, by being absent from the dinner table, but he arranged to come in afterwards to exchange the napkins. He probably put the poisoned napkin into the clothes he discarded. As for motive, long-standing hatred might be enough, but he is also somebody who knew that he would benefit handsomely when Acrise died ... stop him, will you?'

But the General, with a tackle reminiscent of the days when he had been the best wing three-quarter in the country, had already brought to the floor Lord Acrise's secretary, Snewin.

The Four Seasons

Michael Innes

The archdeacon had told us a ghost story, and as the polite murmurs of interest and appreciation died away our hostess threw a log in the fire. It was quite a small log, but nevertheless the action committed us to a further sleepy, even if very tolerably comfortable half-hour. And this prompted one of the younger people to a question, the precise phrasing of which was perhaps a shade lacking in tact, 'And now,' she asked, 'couldn't we have a really exciting one?'

'A mystery story,' another girl said. 'A murder in a sealed room, and then some frightfully cunning detection, and all ending up in a terribly thrilling chase.'

'That is just what Sir John could give us.' Our hostess turned to Appleby. 'You wouldn't be so unkind as to refuse?'

For a moment the Assistant Commissioner was silent, so that I wondered whether he was going to contrive some polite excuse. A long career at Scotland Yard had provided him with plenty of horrific material, and there had been occasions on which I had known him come out with it forthrightly enough. But he had old-fashioned ideas on what was suitable for mixed company. So I wasn't very surprised by his words when he presently did speak.

'Do you know, I'm afraid that positively nothing in the murderous way comes into my head. But an affair that had its moment of mystery – well, I think I can manage that.'

'Only a moment of it?' The girl who had required excitement was reproachful.

Appleby shook his head. 'Oh – what I shall tell you was abundantly mysterious. But mystery, you know, is another matter. One is lucky ever to get a glimpse of it.' Appleby paused, and it was plain that he spoke seriously. Then he told us his tale.

'John and Elizabeth Fray were old friends of my wife's family, and for some years we used to spend a week with them just before Christmas. The party would be rather like this one, and the house was similar, too – which is no doubt what has put the incident I am going to describe into my mind. Fray Manor rambled in an easy, unassuming fashion over a good deal of ground and back through several centuries. The oldest bit was undoubtedly at the top. You may judge that to be a good mysterious touch at the start, although I hasten to add that it has no particular relevance for my story.

'Well then, there, at the top of the house, was a fine late-Elizabethan Long Gallery, with a magnificent view through high, grey-mullioned windows. Not your sort of view, though. Fray is in the Fen Country; and the house looks out over level fields stretching to the horizon, with here and there a canal or windmill or church tower, and everywhere an enormous sky.

'But there was another particular in which the set-up at Fray isn't to be compared with this.' And here Appleby turned to our hostess with a smile. 'Neither John nor Elizabeth had the sort of grasp you and Hugh possess of family history – and particularly of family possessions. I don't mean that they were indifferent to John's inherit-ance – far from it. But they were vague, and I think felt that through all past and all future time Fray had been and would be the same. In point of fact, there were ominous signs that they were mistaken, and the family fortunes were altogether shakier than they understood.

'I used to doubt whether their small son, Robin, would much mend matters. For Robin too was vague – although in what might be called a potentially more distinguished way. He was a shy child, but with some hidden flame in him – of passion, of imagination: one couldn't tell what. Certainly he was more likely to add something to the ideal than to the practical world. I'm afraid that I can't describe him better than that – which is a pity, since my story turns on him.'

'Robin Fray is its hero?' The Archdeacon asked this. And Appleby nodded. 'Yes. Not, I'm glad to say, the tragic hero. Although in a sense, it was a near thing.'

'I don't need to tell you much about the house-party. It wasn't large, and we nearly all were friends of long standing. But there were three exceptions. Miss Shibley was an elderly woman who painted dogs, and John Fray's admiration for this accomplishment was so great that he had made Elizabeth invite her to stop, pretty well out of the blue. Then there was a fellow called Habgood, who appeared to do free-lance articles on country houses for the magazines. Finally, and in rather a different category, there was an American cousin, Charles Fray.

'The actual cousinship must have been extremely remote, since the American branch of the family had been established in New England for many generations. But I was amused to notice that Charles knew far more about the family history than John did. Not that Charles obtruded his knowledge. He was an observant, rather diffident bachelor. It was with some surprise that I gathered he was a highly successful business executive and extremely wealthy. He was due to conclude his visit a couple of days after my own arrival. I was sorry about this, because he seemed to me a thoroughly nice fellow.

'I've mentioned the Long Gallery. We had tea there on the last afternoon of Charles Fray's stay, and it happened that he and I made a little tour of inspection of the paintings lining one side of the place. There were a great many of them, although if Frays had ever had luck on their continental wanderings, and brought home a Titian or a Rubens, it had long since gone to the sale room. But there is often a mild charm in a collection of mediocre pictures that have accreted over some centuries in that sort of house, and my American acquaintance was clearly delighted with this record of his English relatives' artistic tastes.

'There was one painting in particular that he paused before. For some moments I couldn't see why. It was a small autumnal landscape with figures, executed in the Flemish taste of the late sixteenth century, which would have been pleasing enough if the quality of the painting hadn't been rather notably poor. What was represented was a bleak, level scene with a windmill in the middle distance and the towers of a tiny town closing the horizon. In the foreground was the gable of a house, with an attic window out of which a small boy was gazing rather disconsolately at the prospect. I had just taken this in when

Charles Fray touched my arm and pointed across the Gallery. I saw his point. There, through the large Tudor window, was an actual landscape very like the painted one we had been glancing at. It was possible to guess at once what had prompted some bygone Fray to make this particular purchase. But that, at the moment, wasn't all. At the real window our small friend Robin was himself gazing wistfully out over the bare fields. He and the boy in the picture, one could feel, were both longing for a gorgeous fall of snow.'

Appleby paused on this. The Archdeacon, whose successfully accomplished ghost story gave him the status of a performer who had retired into the wings, judged it proper to offer a word of encouragement. 'A pleasing incident,' he said. 'It makes a picture in itself.'

'No doubt. But it was then handled a shade heavily – chiefly by Miss Shibley, the woman who painted dogs. She came up at that moment, and I pointed out the correspondence that had attracted us. She brought it into general notice, and even teased Robin a little. She asked him if he knew the painting was a magic painting, and that it would never, never snow again outside until it had snowed in the painting first. It would have been difficult to tell what Robin made of this. I thought Charles Fray looked a little startled, and that at the same time he was watching the child curiously. Then he turned the conversation by asking John whether he knew anything about the origin of the Flemish painting.

'But John, of course, was as vague as usual. He had once been told some story about it, which had entirely gone out of his head. He did remember that when his father died there had been some reason for having it specially looked at by the fellow who came down and valued everything. It hadn't proved to be worth much.

'Habgood, the guest who went round writing up country houses, took a hand at this point. That is to say, he peered at the painting with a good deal of curiosity, and then rather baldly remarked that its owner was certainly right, and that it was artistically worthless. I believe John Fray was slightly nettled; probably he liked the thing just because it had a smack of his own familiar landscape; and the incident was closed by some other guest having the good sense to cause a diversion.

'The next morning Charles Fray took his departure. I remember him looking up at the sky as he prepared to step into his car, and saying – in rather a whimsical tone – something about snow coming soon. It was true that that great sky appeared heavy with it. But certainly not a flake had fallen.

'And now I come to the sudden crisis of the affair. What remained of the party was gathered in the drawing-room shortly after lunch when Robin burst in upon us like a small madman. "It's come!" he shouted. "It's come, it's come, it's come!" His eyes were blazing, and as he stared at us it happened that for a second I met his gaze directly. You remember my saying that there was a moment not simply of the mysterious, but of mystery, in the business? Well, this was it. The boy had met a mystery. He had met the real thing. And he was exalted.

'But now his mother was pulling him up – gently enough, but decidedly. "Robin dear, don't be so noisy. And what has come?"

'"The snow. It's come, I tell you!"

'I think we all turned and looked through the window. The sky was more leaden than ever – but still no snow was falling. And suddenly, the boy laughed – quite wildly. "Sillies!" he shouted. "Dear old sillies! Not outside. In the picture. Don't you remember? It *has* to be in the picture –"

'There was an awkward silence. Some of us, I imagine, borne of us, I imagine, supposed the child to be delirious, and the more obtuse may have concluded that it was all some sort of impertinent joke. I could see Robin's parents exchange an alarmed glance. They were simple souls remember, and probably regarded their boy as being at best dangerously dreamy and fanciful.

'Habgood was the first person to produce what looked like a sensible reaction. "I suppose," he said, "that somebody may have been perpetrating a trick up there? I'll go and see." And then he turned to Robin. "There's often a good deal of magic in pictures, you know. But it doesn't always last." He gave the boy a kindly pat on the shoulder, and left the room.

'For some seconds we were all silent. And then somebody gave a little involuntary exclamation, and pointed to the window. The first flakes were coming down.'

Our hostess gave a deft kick at her small log, and flame flickered up around it. 'I hope,' she said, 'there *was* magic in the picture.'

Appleby nodded. 'I was hoping so, too. And I was in possession, you know, of an important piece of evidence.'

'Evidence?'

'Just that single glance of the boy's. To a policeman, a wink – or call it the absolute absence of one – ought to be as good as a nod, any day. Somehow it suddenly struck us that we'd all better follow Habgood up to the Long Gallery. I said so, pretty vigorously – and then led the way, with Robin's hand in mine.

'As we mounted the final flight of stairs, Habgood came down to meet us. He glanced at the boy, and for a moment he just didn't appear to know what to say. It was uncomfortable, as you may guess. And then he found what wasn't a bad tone – light, but not in the least condescending or facetious. "It's gone. Robin. It's gone, as it came. It's true, isn't it, that all snow doesn't lie?"

'The boy said nothing, but I felt his hand tremble, and I saw that he had gone very pale. Suddenly he gave a tug; I let him go; and he ran to the far end of the Gallery where the picture hung. By the time he got to the end of that long vista he looked quite comically – or tragically – small.

'When we came up with him he was very still, gazing at the familiar, the mediocre, the untransformed autumnal painting – hanging as it had always hung on the known, predictable wall. He seemed to have no disposition to cry, and for a moment nobody had anything to say. Then some worthy woman began talking nervously to Elizabeth Fray about tricks of light, and what a charming fancy of Robin's it had been. Outside, the snow was still falling.

'I looked at the little painting, and suddenly I was quite sure that there should indeed be snow there too. This wasn't entirely intuition. I had, in fact, been doing my best to think. And now I asked John Fray to close the doors at either end of the Gallery, and to let nobody out. Then I searched the place – pretty grimly, for I had a notion that, so far as the boy's confidence in this universe was concerned, rather a lot depended on it. Of course there hadn't been time to find a really cunning hiding-place. Within half-an-hour, Robin had his snow-scene in his hands.'

The girl who had wanted a sealed room and a thrilling chase cried out delightedly at this. 'Really and truly?'

Appleby smiled at her. 'Really and truly. There it was: the same landscape, the same attic window, the same small boy. But everywhere, snow. And such snow! Teniers couldn't have done it. Nor could he have done the figures with which the small landscape was peopled. Against that snow their life was miraculous. What Robin Fray held was, in its minor way, a masterpiece. Which is what, from the elder Breughel, you might expect.'

Appleby had paused. 'Explanations? Well, not many are needed. What had prompted Miss Shibley to her joke about the picture being transformed into a snow-scene? The subconscious memory of a bit of art-history gathered in her student days. What had sent Habgood, the only man with any sort of connoisseurship, to the Long Gallery, before anybody else could check up on Robin's apparently fantastic story? Fuller knowledge of the same bit of history. That was as much as I could obscurely guess while the episode was taking place.

Now I can add what I discovered later.

'Breughel is believed to have painted four companion pictures: an identical scene, but at the four seasons of the year *Spring* and *Summer* survive – the first in Hungary and the second in a public collection in New York. Long ago, a Fray came into possession *of Autumn*. But his grandson – it was long before a Pieter Breughel was accounted very valuable – gave it away to a friend who fancied it, but first caused a mediocre copy to be made by an itinerant painter from the Low Countries. No doubt he wanted some record of a landscape that a little recalled his own estate. Later still, the original *Autumn* perished in a fire. The copy that remained at Fray had, of course, no more than historical interest or value; nobody would give more than a few hundred pounds for it at the most.

'The fourth painting, *Winter*, had long been thought to have perished. But Charles Fray, who was a collector, had run it to earth somewhere. Knowing that the English Frays had once owned the original *Autumn*, he brought *Winter* with him on his visit, intending it as a parting gift – a princely gift – to his kinsman and to the home of his ancestors. Miss Shibley's joke prompted him to substitute it for the old copy of *Autumn* just before leaving. The old copy of *Autumn* itself he simply left leaning against the wall. The situation, he supposed, would thus at once explain itself, and at the same time give Robin, to whom he had taken a great fancy, a little amusement.

'So you see what happened. As soon as Robin tumbled in on us with his story, Habgood realised that *Winter* had turned up – and that if he could make off with it when only Robin had seen it, the boy would simply be disbelieved. Things might, of course, go wrong if Charles Fray made inquiries. But if Charles got no acknowledgement of his gift from his English kinsman he would almost certainly remain silent; and if *Winter* was subsequently heard of on the market he would presume that John Fray was behind the sale. Habgood was astute.'

Our hostess considered. 'But not at all nice. What happened to *Winter*?'

'It hangs in Robin Fray's bedroom now. And I don't think he'll ever have to sell it. The benevolent transatlantic cousin has been around again, and Robin looks like being his heir.'

No Sanity Clause

Ian Rankin

It was all Edgar Allan Poe's fault. Either that or the Scottish Parliament. Joey Briggs was spending most of his days in the run-up to Christmas sheltering from Edinburgh's biting December winds. He'd been walking up George IV Bridge one day and had watched a down-and-out slouching into the Central Library. Joey had hesitated. He wasn't a down-and-out, not yet anyway. Maybe he would be soon, if Scully Aitchison MSP got his way, but for now Joey had a bedsit and a trickle of state cash. Thing was, nothing made you miss money more than Christmas. The shop windows displayed their magnetic pull. There were queues at the cash machines. Kids tugged on their parents' sleeves, ready with something new to add to the present list. Boyfriends were out buying gold, while families piled the food trolley high.

And then there was Joey, nine weeks out of prison and nobody to call his friend. He knew there was nothing waiting for him back in his home town. His wife had taken the children and tiptoed out of his life. Joey's sister had written to him in prison with the news. So, eleven months on, Joey had walked through the gates of Saughton Jail and taken the first bus into the city centre, purchased an evening paper and started the hunt for somewhere to live.

The bedsit was fine. It was one of four in a tenement basement just off South Clerk Street, sharing a kitchen and bathroom. The other men worked, didn't say much. Joey's room had a gas fire with a coin-meter beside it, too expensive to keep it going all day. He'd tried sitting in the kitchen with the stove lit, until the landlord had caught him. Then he'd tried steeping in the bath, topping up the hot. But the water always seemed to run cold after half a tub.

'You could try getting a job,' the landlord had said.

Not so easy with a prison record. Most of the jobs were for security and nightwatch. Joey didn't think he'd get very far there.

Following the tramp into the library was one of his better ideas. The uniform behind the desk gave him a look, but didn't say anything. Joey wandered the stacks, picked out a book and sat himself down. And that was that. He became a regular, the staff acknowledged him with a nod and sometimes even a smile. He kept himself presentable, didn't fall asleep the way some of the old guys did. He read for much of the day, alternating between fiction, biographies and textbooks. He read up on local history, plumbing and Winston Churchill, Nigel Tranter's novels and National Trust gardens. He knew the library would close over Christmas, didn't know what he'd do without it. He never borrowed books, because he was afraid they'd have him on some blacklist: convicted housebreaker and petty thief, not to be trusted with loan material.

He dreamt of spending Christmas in one of the town's posh hotels, looking out across Princes Street Gardens to the Castle. He'd order room service and watch TV. He'd take as many baths as he liked. They'd clean his clothes for him and return them to the room. He dreamt of the presents he'd buy himself: a big radio with a CD player, some new shirts and pairs of shoes; and books. Plenty of books.

The dream became almost real to him, so that he found himself nodding off in the library, coming to as his head hit the page he'd been reading. Then he'd have to concentrate, only to find himself drifting into a warm sleep again.

Until he met Edgar Allan Poe.

It was a book of poems and short stories, among them

'The Purloined Letter'. Joey loved that, thought it was really clever the way you could hide something by putting it right in front of people. Something that didn't look out of place, people would just ignore it. There'd been a guy in Saughton, doing time for fraud. He'd told Joey: 'Three things: a suit, a haircut and an expensive watch. If you've got those, it's amazing what you can get away with.' He'd meant that clients had trusted him, because they'd seen something they were comfortable with, something they expected to see. What they hadn't seen was what was right in front of their noses, to wit: a shark, someone who was going to take a big bite out of their savings.

As Joey's eyes flitted back over Poe's story, he started to get an idea. He started to get what he thought was a very good idea indeed. Problem was, he needed what the fraudster had called 'the start-up', meaning some cash. He happened to look across to where one of the old tramps was slumped on a chair, the newspaper in front of him unopened. Joey looked around: nobody was watching. The place was dead: who had time to go to the library when Christmas was around the corner? Joey walked over to the old guy, slipped a hand into his coat pocket. Felt coins and notes, bunched his fingers around them. He glanced down at the newspaper. There was a story about Scully Aitchison's campaign. Aitchison was the MSP who wanted all offenders put on a central register, open to public inspection. He said law-abiding folk had the right to know if their neighbour was a thief or a murderer – as if stealing was the same as killing somebody! There was a small photo of Aitchison, too, beaming that self-satisfied smile, his glasses glinting. If Aitchison got his way, Joey would never get out of the rut.

Not unless his plan paid off.

John Rebus saw his girlfriend kissing Santa Claus. There was a German Market in Princes Street Gardens. That was where Rebus was to meet Jean. He hadn't expected to find her in a clinch with a man dressed in a red suit, black boots and snowy-white beard. Santa broke away and moved off, just as Rebus was approaching. German folk songs were blaring out. There was a startled look on Jean's face.

'What was that all about?' he asked.

'I don't know.' She was watching the retreating figure. 'I think maybe he's just had too much festive spirit. He came up and grabbed me.' Rebus made to follow, but Jean stopped him. 'Come on, John. Season of goodwill and all that.'

'It's assault, Jean.'

She laughed, regaining her composure. 'You're going to take St Nicholas down the station and put him in the cells?' She rubbed his arm. 'Let's forget it, eh? The fun starts in ten minutes.'

Rebus wasn't too sure that the evening was going to be 'fun'. He spent every day bogged down in crimes and tragedies. He wasn't sure that a 'mystery dinner' was going to offer much relief. It had been Jean's idea. There was a hotel just across the road. You all went in for dinner, were handed envelopes telling you which character you'd be playing. A body was discovered, and then you all turned detective.

'It'll be fun,' Jean insisted, leading him out of the gardens. She had three shopping bags with her. He wondered if any of them were for him. She'd asked for a list of his Christmas wants, but so far all he'd come up with were a couple of CDs by String Driven Thing.

As they entered the hotel, they saw that the mystery evening was being held on the mezzanine floor. Most of the guests had already gathered and were enjoying glasses of cava. Rebus asked in vain for a beer.

'Cava's included in the price,' the waitress told him. A man dressed in Victorian costume was checking names and handing out carrier bags.

'Inside,' he told Jean and Rebus, 'you'll find instructions, a secret clue that only you know, your name, and an item of clothing.'

'Oh,' Jean said, 'I'm Little Nell.' She fixed a bonnet to her head. 'Who are you, John?'

'Mr Bumble.' Rebus produced his name tag and a

yellow woolen scarf, which Jean insisted on tying around his neck.

'It's a Dickensian theme, specially for Christmas,' the host revealed, before moving off to confront his other victims. Everyone looked a bit embarrassed, but most were trying for enthusiasm. Rebus didn't doubt that a couple of glasses of wine over dinner would loosen a few Edinburgh stays. There were a couple of faces he recognised. One was a journalist, her arm around her boyfriend's waist. The other was a man who appeared to be with his wife. He had one of those looks to him, the kind that says you should know him. She was blonde and petite and about a decade younger than her husband.

'Isn't that an MSP?' Jean whispered. 'His name's Scully Aitchison,' Rebus told her. Jean was reading her information sheet. 'The victim tonight is a certain Ebenezer Scrooge,' she said. 'And did you kill him?'

She thumped his arm. Rebus smiled, but his eyes were on the MSP. Aitchison's face was bright red. Rebus guessed he'd been drinking since lunchtime. His voice boomed across the floor, broadcasting the news that he and Catriona had booked a room for the night, so they wouldn't have to drive back to the constituency.

They were all mingling on the mezzanine landing. The room where they'd dine was just off to the right, its doors still closed. Guests were starting to ask each other which characters they were playing. As one elderly lady – Miss Havisham on her name tag – came over to ask Jean about Little Nell, Rebus saw a red-suited man appear at the top of the stairs. Santa carried what looked like a half-empty sack. He started making his way across the floor, but was stopped by Aitchison.

'*J'accuse!*' the MSP bawled. 'You killed Scrooge because of his inhumanity to his fellow man!' Aitchison's wife came to the rescue, dragging her husband away, but Santa's eyes seemed to follow them. As he made to pass Rebus, Rebus fixed him with a stare.

'Jean,' he asked, 'is he the same one …?'

She only caught the back of Santa's head. 'They all look alike to me,' she said.

Santa was on his way to the next flight of stairs. Rebus watched him leave, then turned back to the other guests, all of them now tricked out in odd items of clothing. No wonder Santa had looked like he'd stumbled into an asylum. Rebus was reminded of a Marx Brothers line, Groucho trying to get Chico's name on a contract, telling him to sign the sanity clause.

But, as Chico said, everyone knew there was no such thing as Sanity Clause.

Joey jimmied open his third room of the night. The Santa suit had worked a treat. Okay, so it was hot and uncomfortable, and the beard was itching his neck, but it worked! He'd breezed through reception and up the stairs. So far, as he'd worked the corridors all he'd had were a few jokey comments. No one from security asking him who he was. No guests becoming suspicious. He fitted right in, and he was right under their noses.

God bless Edgar Allan Poe.

The woman in the fancy dress shop had even thrown in a sack, saying he'd be wanting to fill it. How true: in the first bedroom, he'd dumped out the crumpled sheets of old newspaper and started filling the sack – clothes, jewellery, the contents of the mini-bar. Same with the second room: a tap on the door to make sure no one was home, then the chisel into the lock and hey presto. Thing was, there wasn't much in the rooms. A notice in the wardrobe told clients to lock all valuables in the hotel safe at reception. Still, he had a few nice things: camera, credit cards, bracelet and necklace. Sweat was running into his eyes, but he couldn't afford to shed his disguise. He was starting to have crazy thoughts: take a good long soak; ring down for room service; find a room that hadn't been taken and settle in for the duration. In the third room, he sat on the bed, feeling dizzy. There was a briefcase open beside him, just lots of paperwork. His stomach growled, and he remembered that his last meal had been a Mars Bar supper the previous day. He broke open a jar of salted peanuts, switched the TV on while he ate. As he put the empty jar down, he happened to glance at the contents of the brief-case. 'Parliamentary briefing ... Law and Justice Sub-Committee ...' He saw a list of names on the top sheet. One of them was coloured with a yellow marker. Scully Aitchison.

The drunk man downstairs ... That was where Joey knew him from! He leapt to his feet, trying to think. He could stay here and give the MSP a good hiding. He could ... He picked up the room-service menu, called down and ordered smoked salmon, a steak, a bottle each of best red wine and malt whisky. Then heard himself saying those sweetest words: 'Put it on my room, will you?'

Then he settled back to wait. Flipped through the paper-work again. An envelope slipped out. Card inside, and a letter inside the card.

Dear Scully, it began. *I hope it isn't all my fault, this idea of yours for a register of offenders ...*

'I haven't a clue,' said Rebus.

Nor did he. Dinner was over, the actor playing Scrooge was flat out on the mezzanine floor, and Rebus was as far away from solving the crime as ever. Thankfully, a bar had been opened up, and he spent most of his time perched on a high stool, pretending to read the background notes while taking sips of beer. Jean had hooked up with Miss Havisham, while Aitchison's wife was slumped in one of the armchairs, drawing on a cigarette. The MSP himself was playing ringmaster, and had twice confronted Rebus, calling for him to reveal himself as the villain.

'Innocent, m'lud,' was all Rebus had said.

'We think it's Magwitch,' Jean said, suddenly breathless by Rebus's side, her bonnet at a jaunty angle. 'He and Scrooge knew one another in prison.'

'I didn't know Scrooge served time,' Rebus said.

'That's because you're not asking questions.'

'I don't need to; I've got you to tell me. That's what makes a good detective.'

He watched her march away. Four of the diners had encircled the poor man playing Magwitch. Rebus had harboured suspicions, too ... but now he was thinking of jail time, and how it affected those serving it. It gave them a certain look, a look they brought back into the world on their release. The same look he'd seen in Santa's eyes.

And here was Santa now, coming back down the stairs, his sack slung over one shoulder. Crossing the mezzanine floor as if seeking someone out. Then finding them: Scully Aitchison. Rebus rose from his stool and wandered over.

'Have you been good this year?' Santa was asking Aitchison. 'No worse than anyone else,' the MSP smirked.

'Sure about that?' Santa's eyes narrowed.

'I wouldn't lie to Father Christmas.'

'What about this plan of yours, the offender register?' Aitchison blinked a couple of times. 'What about it?'

Santa held a piece of paper aloft, his voice rising. 'Your own nephew's serving time for fraud. Managed to keep that quiet, haven't you?'

Aitchison stared at the letter. 'Where in hell …? How …?' The journalist stepped forward. 'Mind if I take a look?' Santa handed over the letter, then pulled off his hat and beard. Started heading for the stairs down. Rebus blocked his way.

'Time to hand out the presents,' he said quietly. Joey looked at him and understood immediately, slid the sack from his shoulder. Rebus took it. 'Now on you go.'

'You're not arresting me?'

'Who'd feed Dancer and Prancer?' Rebus asked.

His stomach full of steak and wine, a bottle of malt in the capacious pocket of his costume, Joey smiled his way back towards the outside world.

The Footprint in the Sky

John Dickson Carr

She awoke out of confused dreams; awoke with a start, and lay staring at the white ceiling of her bedroom for a minute or two before she could convince herself it was anything but a dream. But it was a dream.

The cold, brittle sunlight poured in at the open window. The cold, brittle air, blowing the curtains, stirred a light coating of snow on the window-sill. It stirred briskly in that little, bare room; it should have set the blood racing, and Dorothy Brant breathed it deeply.

Everything was all right. She was at the country cottage, where she and Dad and Harry had come down for the skating on the frozen lake; possibly even a little mild skiing, if the snow came on according to the weather forecast. And the snow had fallen. She should have been glad of that, though for some reason the sight of it on the window-sill struck her with a kind of terror.

Shivering in the warm bed, the clothes pulled up about her chin, she looked at the little clock on her bedside. Twenty minutes past nine. She had overslept; and Dad and Harry would be wanting their breakfast. Again she told herself that everything was all right: though now, fully awake, she knew it was not. The unpleasantness of yesterday returned. Mrs Topham next door – that old shrew and thief as well ...

It was the only thing which could have marred this weekend. They had looked forward to the skating: the crisp blades thudding and ringing on the ice, the flight, the long scratching drag as you turned, the elm-trees black against a clear cold sky. But there was Mrs Topham with her stolen watch and her malicious good manners, huddled up in the cottage next door and spoiling everything.

Put it out of your mind! No good brooding over it: put it out of your mind!

Dorothy Brant braced herself and got out of bed, reaching for her dressing-gown and slippers. But it was not only her dressing-gown she found draped across the chair; it was her heavy fur coat. And there were a pair of soft-leather slippers. They were a pair of soft-leather moccasins, ornamented with bead-work, which Harry had brought her back from the States; but now the undersides were cold, damp, and stiff, almost frozen. That was when a subconscious fear struck at her, took possession, and would not leave.

Closing the window, she padded out to the bathroom. The small cottage, with its crisp white curtains and smell of old wood, was so quiet that she could hear voices talking downstairs. It was a mumble in which no words were distinguishable: Harry's quick tenor, her father's slower and heavier voice, and another she could not identify, but which was slowest and heaviest of all.

What was wrong? She hurried through her bath and through her dressing. Not only were they up but they must be getting their own breakfast, for she could smell coffee boiling. And she was very slow; in spite of nine hours' sleep she felt as edgy and washed-out as though she had been up all night.

Giving a last jerk of the comb through her brown bobbed hair, putting on no powder or lipstick, she ran downstairs. At the door of the living-room she stopped abruptly. Inside were her father, her cousin Harry, and the local Superintendent of Police.

'Good morning, miss,' said the Superintendent.

She never forgot the look of that little room or the look on the faces of those in it. Sunlight poured into it, touching the bright-coloured rough-woven rugs, the rough stone fireplace. Through side windows she could see out across the snow-covered lawn to where – twenty yards away and separated from them only by a tall laurel hedge, with a gateway – was Mrs Topham's white weatherboarded cottage.

But what struck her with a shock of alarm as she came into the room was the sense of a conversation suddenly cut off; the look she surprised on their faces when they glanced round, quick and sallow, as a camera might have surprised it.

'Good morning, miss,' repeated Superintendent Mason saluting.

Harry Ventnor intervened, in a kind of agony. His naturally high colour was higher still; even his large feet and bulky shoulders, his small sinewy hands, looked agitated.

'Don't say anything, Dolly!' he urged. 'Don't say anything! They can't make you say anything. Wait until –'

'I certainly think –' began her father slowly. He looked down his nose, and then along the side of his pipe, everywhere except at Dorothy. 'I certainly think,' he went on, clearing his throat, 'that it would be as well not to speak hastily until –'

'If you please, sir,' said Superintendent Mason, clearing his throat. 'Now, miss, I'm afraid I must ask you some questions. But it is my duty to tell you that you need not answer my questions until you have seen your solicitor.'

'Solicitor? But I don't want a solicitor. What on earth should I want with a solicitor?'

Superintendent Mason looked meaningly at her father and Harry Ventnor, as though bidding them to mark that.

'It's about Mrs Topham, miss.'

'Oh!'

'Why do you say "Oh"?'

'Go on, please. What is it?'

'I understand, miss, that you and Mrs Topham had "words" yesterday? A bit of a dust-up, like?'

'Yes, you could certainly call it that.'

'May I ask what about?'

'I'm sorry,' said Dorothy; 'I can't tell you that. It would only give the old cat an opportunity to say I had been slandering her. So that's it! What has she been telling you?'

'Why, miss,' said Superintendent Mason, taking out a pencil and scratching the side of his jaw with it, 'I'm afraid she's not exactly in a condition to tell us anything. She's in a nursing-home at Guildford, rather badly smashed up round the head. Just between ourselves, it's touch and go whether she'll recover.'

First Dorothy could not feel her heart beating at all, and then it seemed to pound with enormous rhythm. The Superintendent was looking at her steadily. She forced herself to say:

'You mean she's had an accident?'

'Not exactly, miss. The doctor says she was hit three or four times with that big glass paper-weight you may have seen on the table at her cottage. Eh?'

'You don't mean – you don't mean somebody *did* it? Deliberately? But who did it?'

'Well, miss,' said Superintendent Mason, looking at her still harder until he became a huge Puritan face with a small mole beside his nose. 'I'm bound to tell you that by everything we can see so far, it looks as though you did it.'

This wasn't happening. It couldn't be. She afterwards remembered, in a detached kind of way, studying all of them: the little lines round Harry's eyes in the sunlight, the hastily brushed light hair, the loose leather wind-jacket whose zip fastener was half undone. She remembered thinking that despite his athletic prowess he looked ineffectual and a little foolish. But then her own father was not of much use now.

She heard her own voice.

'But that's absurd!'

'I hope so, miss. I honestly hope so. Now tell me: were you out of this house last night?'

'When?'

'At any time.'

'Yes. No. I don't know. Yes, I think I was.'

'For God's sake, Dolly,' said her father, 'don't say

anything more until we've got a lawyer here. I've tele-phoned to town; I didn't want to alarm you; I didn't even wake you: there's some explanation of this. There must be!'

It was not her own emotion; it was the wretchedness of his face which held her. Bulky, semi-bald, worried about business, worried about everything else in this world, that was John Brant. His crippled left arm and black glove were pressed against his side. He stood in the bright pool of sunlight, a face of misery.

'I've – seen her,' he explained. 'It wasn't pretty, that wasn't. Not that I haven't seen worse. In the war.' He touched his arm. 'But you're a little girl, Dolly; you're only a little girl. You couldn't have done that.'

His plaintive tone asked for confirmation.

'Just one moment, sir,' interposed Superintendent Mason. 'Now, miss! You tell me you *were* outside the house last night?'

'Yes.'

'In the snow?'

'Yes, yes, yes!'

'Do you remember the time?'

'No, I don't think so.'

'Tell me, miss: what size shoes do you wear?'

'Four.'

'That's a rather small size, isn't it?' When she nodded

dumbly, Superintendent Mason shut up his notebook. 'Now, if you'll just come with me?'

The cottage had a side door. Without putting his fingers on the knob, Mason twisted the spindle round and opened it. The overhang of the eaves had kept clear the two steps leading down; but beyond a thin coating of snow lay like a plaster over the world between here and the shuttered cottage across the way.

There were two strings of footprints in that snow. Dorothy knew whose they were. Hardened and sharp printed, one set of prints moved out snakily from the steps, passed under the arch of the powdered laurel hedge, and stopped at the steps to the side door of Mrs Topham's house. Another set of the same tracks – a little blurred, spaced at longer intervals where the person had evidently been running desperately – came back from the cottage to these steps.

That mute sign of panic stirred Dorothy's memory. It wasn't a dream. She had done it. Subconsciously she had known it all the time. She could remember other things: the fur coat clasped round her pyjamas, the sting of the snow to wet slippers, the blind rush in the dark.

'Yours, miss?' inquired Superintendent Mason.

'Yes. Oh, yes, they're mine.'

'Easy, miss,' muttered the Superintendent. 'You're looking a bit white round the gills. Come in here and sit down; I won't hurt you.' Then his own tone grew petulant. Or perhaps something in the heavy simplicity of the girl's manner penetrated his official bearing. 'But why did you do it, miss? Lord, why did you do it? That's to say, breaking open that desk of hers to get a handful of trinkets not worth ten quid for the lot? And then not even taking the trouble to mess up your footprints afterwards!' He coughed, checking himself abruptly.

John Brant's voice was acid. 'Good, my friend. Very good. The first sign of intelligence so far. I presume you don't suggest my daughter is insane?'

'No, sir. But they were her mother's trinkets, I hear.'

'Where did you hear that? You, I suppose, Harry?' Harry Ventnor pulled up the zip fastener of his wind-jacket as though girding himself. He seemed to suggest that he was the good fellow whom everybody was persecuting; that he wanted to be friends with the world, if they would only let him. Yet such sincerity blazed in his small features that it was difficult to doubt his good intentions.

'Now look here, Dad, old boy. I *had* to tell them, didn't I? It's no good trying to hide things like that. I know that, just from reading those stories –'

'Stories!'

'All right: say what you like. They always find out, and then they make it worse than it really was.' He let this sink in. 'I tell you, you're going about it in the wrong way. Suppose Dolly did have a row with the Topham about that jewellery? Suppose she *did* go over there last night? Suppose those are her footprints? Does that prove she bashed the Topham? Not that a public service wasn't done; but why couldn't it have been a burglar just as well?'

Superintendent Mason shook his head.

'Because it couldn't, sir.'

'But why? I'm asking you, why?'

'There's no harm in telling you that, sir, if you'll just listen. You probably remember that it began to snow last night at a little past eleven o'clock.'

'No, I don't. We were all in bed by then.'

'Well, you can take my word for it,' Mason told him patiently. 'I was up half the night at the police station; and it did. It stopped snowing about midnight. You'll have to take my word for that too, but we can easily prove it. You see, sir, Mrs Topham was alive and in very good health at well after midnight. I know that too, because she rang up the police station and said she was awake and nervous and thought there were burglars in the neighbourhood. Since the lady does that same thing,' he explained with a certain grimness, 'on the average of about three times a month, I don't stress *that*. What I am telling you is that her call came in at 12.10, at least ten minutes after the snow had stopped.'

Harry hesitated, and the Superintendent went on with the same patient air:

'Don't you see it, sir? Mrs Topham wasn't attacked until after the snow stopped. Round her cottage now there's twenty yards of clean, clear, unmarked snow in every direction. The only marks in that snow, the only marks of any kind at all, are the footprints Miss Brant admits she made herself.'

Then he rose at them in exasperation.

"Tisn't as though anybody else could have made the tracks. Even if Miss Brant didn't admit it herself, I'm absolutely certain nobody else did. You, Mr Ventnor, wear size ten shoes. Mr Brant wears size nine. Walk in size four tracks? Ayagh! And yet somebody did get into that cottage with a key, bashed the old lady pretty murderously, robbed her desk, and got away again. If there are no other tracks or marks of any kind in the snow, who did it? Who must have done it?'

Dorothy could consider it, now, in almost a detached way. She remembered the paper-weight with which Mrs Topham had been struck. It lay on the table in Mrs Topham's stuffy parlour, a heavy glass globe with a tiny landscape inside. When you shook the glass globe, a miniature snowstorm rose within – which seemed to make the attack more horrible.

She wondered if she had left any fingerprints on it. But over everything rose Renée Topham's face, Renée Topham, her mother's bosom friend.

'I hated her,' said Dorothy; and, unexpectedly, she began to cry.

Dennis Jameson, of the law firm of Morris, Farnsworth & Jameson, Lincoln's Inn Fields, shut up his briefcase with a snap. He was putting on his hat and coat when Billy Farnsworth looked into the office.

'Hullo!' said Farnsworth. 'You off to Surrey over that Brant business?'

'Yes.'

'H'm. Believe in miracles, do you?'

'No.'

'That girl's guilty, my lad. You ought to know that.'

'It's our business,' said Jameson, 'to do what we can for our clients.'

Farnsworth looked at him shrewdly. 'I see it in your ruddy cheek. Quixotry is alive again. Young idealist storms to relief of good-looker in distress, swearing to –'

'I've met her twice,' said Jameson. 'I like her, yes. But, merely using a small amount of intelligence on this, I can't see that they've got such a thundering good case against her.'

'Oh, my lad!'

'Well, look at it. What do they say the girl did? This Mrs Topham was struck several times with a glass paper-weight. There are no fingerprints on the paper-weight, which shows signs of having been wiped. But, after having the forethought to wipe her fingerprints carefully off the paper-weight, Dorothy Brant then walks back to her cottage and leaves behind two sets of footprints which could be seen by aerial observation a mile up. Is that reasonable?'

Farnsworth looked thoughtful.

'Maybe they would say she isn't reasonable,' he pointed out. 'Never mind the psychology. What you've got to get round are the physical facts. Here is the mysterious widow Topham entirely alone in the house; the only servant comes in by day. Here are one person's footprints. Only that girl could have made the tracks: and, in fact, admits she did. It's a physical impossibility for anybody else to have entered or left the house. How do you propose to get round that?'

'I don't know,' said Jameson rather hopelessly. 'But I want to hear her side of it first. The only thing nobody seems to have heard, or even to be curious about, is what she thinks herself.'

Yet, when he met her at the cottage late that afternoon, she cut the ground from under his feet.

Twilight was coming down when he turned in at the gate, a bluish twilight in which the snow looked grey. Jameson stopped a moment at the gate, and stared across at the thin laurel hedge dividing this property from Mrs

Topham's. There was nothing remarkable about this hedge, which was some six feet high and cut through by a gateway like a Gothic arch. But in front of the arch, peering up at the snow-coated side of the hedge just above it, stood a large figure in cap and waterproof. Somehow he looked familiar. At his elbow another man, evidently the local Superintendent of Police, was holding up a camera; and a flash-bulb glared against the sky. Though he was too far away to hear anything, Jameson had a queer impression that the large man was laughing uproariously.

Harry Ventnor, whom he knew slightly, met Jameson at the door.

'She's in there,' Harry explained, nodding towards the front room. 'Er – don't upset her, will you? Here, what the devil are they doing with that hedge?'

He stared across the lawn.

'Upset her?' said Jameson with some asperity. 'I'm here, if possible, to help her. Won't you or Mr Brant give some assistance? Do you honestly think that Miss Brant in her rational senses could have done what they say she did?'

'In her rational senses?' repeated Harry. After looking at Jameson in a curious way, he said no more; he turned abruptly and hurried off across the lawn.

Yet Dorothy, when Jameson met her, gave no impression of being out of her rational senses. It was her straightforwardness he had always liked, the straight-forwardness which warmed him now. They sat in the homely, firelit room, by the fireplace over which were the silver cups to denote Harry's athletic and gymnastic prowess, and the trophies of John Brant's earlier days at St Moritz. Dorothy herself was an outdoor girl.

'To advise me?' she said. 'You mean, to advise me what to say when they arrest me?'

'Well, they haven't arrested you yet, Miss Brant.'

She smiled at him. 'And yet I'll bet that surprises you, doesn't it? Oh, I know how deeply I'm in! I suppose they're only poking about to get more evidence. And then there's a new man here, a man named March, from Scotland Yard. I feel almost flattered.'

Jameson sat up. He knew now why that immense figure by the hedge had seemed familiar.

'Not Colonel March?'

'Yes. Rather a nice person, really,' answered Dorothy, shading her eyes with her hand. Under her light tone he felt that her nerves were raw. 'Then again, they've been all through my room. And they can't find the watch and the brooch and the rings I'm supposed to have stolen from Aunt Renée Topham. Aunt Renée!'

'So I've heard. But that's the point: what are they getting at? A watch and a brooch and a couple of rings! Why should you steal that from anybody, let alone her?'

'Because they weren't hers,' said Dorothy, suddenly looking up with a white face, and speaking very fast. 'They belonged to my mother.'

'Steady.'

'My mother is dead,' said Dorothy. 'I suppose it wasn't just the watch and the rings, really. That was the excuse, the breaking-point, the thing that brought it on. My mother was a great friend of Mrs Topham. It was "Aunt Renée" this and "Aunt Renée" that, while my mother was alive to pamper her. But my mother wanted me to have those trinkets, such as they were. And Aunt Renée Topham coolly appropriated them, as she appropriates everything else she can. I never knew what had happened to them until yesterday.

'Do you know that kind of woman? Mrs Topham is really charming, aristocratic and charming, with the cool charm that takes all it can get and expects to go on getting it. I know for a fact that she's really got a lot of money, though what she does with it I can't imagine: and the real reason why she buries herself in the country is that she's too mean to risk spending it in town. I never could endure her. Then, when my mother died and I didn't go on pampering Aunt Renée as she thought I should, it was a very difficult thing. How that woman loves to talk about us! Harry's debts, and my father's shaky business. And *me.*'

She checked herself again, smiling at him. 'I'm sorry to inflict all this on you.'

'You're not inflicting anything on me.'

'But it's rather ridiculous, isn't it?'

'Ridiculous,' said Jameson grimly, 'is not the word I should apply to it. So you had a row with her?'

'Oh, a glorious row. A beautiful row. The grandmother of all rows.'

'When?'

'Yesterday. When I saw her wearing my mother's watch.'

She looked at the fire, over which the silver cups glimmered.

'Maybe I said more than I should have,' she went on. 'But I got no support from my father or Harry. I don't blame Dad: he's so worried about business, and that bad arm of his troubles him so much sometimes, that all he wants is peace and quiet. As for Harry, *he* doesn't really like her; but she took rather a fancy to him, and that flatters him. He's a kind of male counterpart of Aunt Renée. Out of a job? – well, depend on somebody else. And I'm in the middle of all this. It's "Dolly, do this," and "Dolly, do that," and "Good old Dolly; she won't mind." But I do mind. When I saw that woman standing there wearing my mother's watch, and saying commiserating things about the fact that we couldn't afford a servant, I felt that something ought to be done about it. So I suppose I must have done something about it.'

Jameson reached out and took her hands. 'All right,' he said. 'Did you do it?'

'I don't know! That's just the trouble.'

'But surely – '

'No. That was one of the things Mrs Topham always had such sport with. You don't know much about anything when you walk in your sleep.'

'Ridiculous, isn't it?' she went on, after another pause. 'Utterly ludicrous. But not to me! Not a bit. Ever since I was a child, when I've been over-tired or nervously exhausted, it's happened. Once I came downstairs and built and lit a fire in the dining-room, and set the table for a meal. I admit it doesn't happen often, and never before with results like this.' She tried to laugh. 'But why do you think my father and Harry looked at me like that? That's the worst of it. I really don't know whether I'm a near-murderer or not.'

This was bad.

Jameson admitted that to himself, even as his reason argued against it. He got up to prowl round the room, and her brown eyes never left him. He could not look away; he saw the tensity of her face in every corner.

'Look here,' he said quietly, 'this is nonsense.'

'Oh, please. Don't you say that. It's not very original.'

'But do you seriously think you went for that woman and still don't know anything about it now?'

'Would it be more difficult than building a fire?'

'I didn't ask you that. *Do* you think you did it?'

'No,' said Dorothy.

That question did it. She trusted him now. There was understanding and sympathy between them, a mental force and communication that could be felt as palpably as the body gives out heat.

'Deep down inside me, no, I don't believe it. I think I should have waked up. And there was no – well, no blood on me, you know. But how are you going to get round the evidence?'

(The evidence. Always the evidence.)

'I did go across there. I can't deny that. I remember half waking up as I was coming back. I was standing in the middle of the lawn in the snow. I had on my fur coat over my pyjamas; I remember feeling snow on my face and my wet slippers under me. I was shivering. And I remember running back. That's all. If I didn't do it, how could anybody else have done it?'

'I beg your pardon,' interposed a new voice. 'Do you mind if, both figuratively and literally, I turn on the light?'

Dennis Jameson knew the owner of that voice. There was the noise of someone fumbling after an electric switch; then, in homely light, Colonel March beamed and basked. Colonel March's seventeen stone was swathed round in a waterproof as big as a tent. He wore a large tweed cap. Under this his speckled face glowed in the cold; and he was smoking, with gurgling relish, the large-bowled pipe which threatened to singe his sandy moustache.

'Ah, Jameson!' he said. He took the pipe out of his mouth and made a gesture with it. 'So it *was* you. I thought I saw you come in. I don't want to intrude; but I think there are at least two things that Miss Brant ought to know.'

Dorothy turned round quickly.

'First,' pursued Colonel March, 'that Mrs Topham is out of danger. She is at least able, like an after-dinner speaker, to say a few words; though with about as much coherence. Second, that out on your lawn there is one of the queerest objects I ever saw in my life.'

Jameson whistled.

'You've met this fellow?' he said to Dorothy. 'He is the head of the Queer Complaints Department. When they come across something outlandish, which may be a hoax or a joke but, on the other hand, may be a serious crime, they shout for him. His mind is so obvious that he hits it every time. To my certain knowledge he has investigated a disappearing room, chased a walking corpse, and found an invisible piece of furniture. If he goes so far as to admit that a thing is a bit unusual, you can look out for squalls.'

Colonel March nodded quite seriously.

'Yes,' he said. 'That is why I am here, you see. They thought we might be interested in that footprint.'

'That footprint?' cried Dorothy. 'You mean – ?'

'No, no; not your footprint, Miss Brant. Another one. Let me explain. I want you, both of you, to look out of that window; I want you to take a look at the laurel hedge between this cottage and the other. The light is almost gone, but study it.'

Jameson went to the window and peered out.

'Well?' he demanded. 'What about it? It's a hedge.'

'As you so shrewdly note, it is a hedge. Now let me ask you a question. Do you think a person could walk along the top of that hedge?'

'Good lord, no!'

'No? Why not?'

'I don't see the joke,' said Jameson, 'but I'll make the proper replies. Because the hedge is only an inch or two thick. It wouldn't support a cat. If you tried to stand on it, you'd come through like a ton of bricks.'

'Quite true. Then what would you say if I told you that someone weighing at least twelve stone must have climbed up the side of it?'

Nobody answered him; the thing was so obviously un-reasonable that nobody could answer. Dorothy Brant and Dennis Jameson looked at each other.

'For,' said Colonel March, 'it would seem that somebody

at least climbed up there. Look at the hedge again. You see the arch cut in it for a gate? Just above that, in the snow along the side of the hedge, there are traces of a footprint. It is a large footprint. I think it can be identified by the heel, though most of it is blurred and sketchy.'

Walking quietly and heavily, Dorothy's father came into the room. He started to speak, but seemed to change his mind at the sight of Colonel March. He went over to Dorothy, who took his arm.

'Then,' insisted Jameson, 'somebody did climb up on the hedge?'

'I doubt it,' said Colonel March. How could he?'

Jameson pulled himself together.

'Look here, sir,' he said quietly. "How could he?" is correct. I never knew you to go on like this without good reason. I know it must have some bearing on the case. But I don't care if somebody climbed up on the hedge. I don't care if he danced the Big Apple on it. The hedge leads nowhere. It doesn't lead to Mrs Topham's; it only divides the two properties. The point is, how did somebody manage to get from here to that other cottage – across sixty feet of un-broken snow – without leaving a trace on it? I ask you that because I'm certain you don't think Miss Brant is guilty.'

Colonel March looked apologetic.

'I know she isn't,' he answered.

In Dorothy Brant's mind was again that vision of the heavy globed paper-weight inside which, as you shook it, a miniature snowstorm arose. She felt that her own wits were being shaken and clouded in the same way.

'I knew Dolly didn't do it,' said John Brant, suddenly putting his arm round his daughter's shoulder. 'I knew that. I told them so. But – '

Colonel March silenced him.

'The real thief, Miss Brant, did not want your mother's watch and brooch and chain and rings. It may interest you to know what he did want. He wanted about fifteen hundred pounds in notes and gold sovereigns, tucked away in that same shabby desk. You seem to have wondered what Mrs Topham did with her money. That is what she did with it. Mrs Topham, by the first words she could get out in semi-consciousness, was merely a common or garden variety of miser. That dull-looking desk in her parlour was the last place any burglar would look for a hoard. Any burglar, that is, except one.'

'Except one?' repeated John Brant, and his eyes seemed to turn inwards.

A sudden ugly suspicion came to Jameson.

'Except one who knew, yes. You, Miss Brant, had the blame deliberately put on you. There was no malice in it. It was simply the easiest way to avoid pain and trouble to the gentleman who did it.

'Now hear what you really did,' said Colonel March, his face darkening. 'You did go out into the snow last night. But you did not go over to Mrs Topham's; and you did not make those two artistic sets of footprints in the snow. When you tell us in your own story that you felt snow sting on your face as well as underfoot, it requires no vast concentration, surely, to realize that the snow was still falling. You went out into it, like many sleep-walkers; you were shocked into semi-consciousness by the snow and the cold air; and you returned long before the end of the snowfall, which covered any real prints you may have made.

'The real thief – who was very much awake – heard you come back and tumble into bed. He saw a heaven-sent opportunity to blame you for a crime you might even think you had committed. He slipped in and took the slippers out of your room. And, when the snow had stopped, he went across to Mrs Topham's. He did not mean to attack her. But she was awake and surprised him; and so, of course, Harry Ventnor struck her down.'

'Harry – '

The word, which Dorothy had said almost at a scream, was checked. She looked round quickly at her father; she stared straight ahead; and then she began to laugh.

'Of course,' said Colonel March. 'As usual, he was letting his (what is it) his "good old Dolly" take the blame.'

A great cloud seemed to have left John Brant; but the fussed and worried look had not left him. He blinked at Colonel March.

'Sir,' he said, 'I would give my good arm to prove what you say. That boy has caused me half the trouble I ever had. But are you raving mad?'

'No.'

'I tell you he couldn't have done it! He's Emily's son, my sister's son. He may be a bad lot; but he's not a magician.'

'You are forgetting,' said Colonel March, 'a certain large size-ten footprint. You are forgetting that interesting sight, a smeared and blurred size-ten footprint on the side of a hedge which would not have held up a cat. A remarkable footprint. A disembodied footprint.'

'But that's the whole trouble,' roared the other. 'The two lines of tracks in the snow were made by a size four shoe. Harry couldn't have made them, any more than I could. It's a physical impossibility. Harry wears size ten. You don't say he could get his feet into flat leather moccasins which would fit my daughter?'

'No,' said Colonel March. 'But he could get his hands into them.'

There was a silence. The Colonel wore a dreamy look; almost a pleased look.

'And in this unusual but highly practical pair of gloves,' he went on, 'Harry Ventnor simply walked across to the other cottage on his hands. No more than that. For a trained gymnast (as those silver cups will indicate) it was nothing. For a rattle-brained gentleman who needed money it was ideal. He crossed in a thin coating of snow, which would show no difference in weight. Doorsteps, cleared of snow by the overhanging roof, protected him at either end when he stood upright. He had endless opportunities to get a key to the side door. Unfortunately, there was that rather low archway in the hedge. Carrying himself on his hands, his feet were curved up and back over the arch of his body to balance him; he blundered, and smeared that disembodied footprint on the side of the hedge. To be quite frank, I am delighted with the device. It is crime upside down; it is leaving a footprint in the sky; it is—'

'A fair cop, sir,' concluded Superintendent Mason, sticking his head in at the door. 'They got him on the other side of Guildford. He must have smelled something wrong when he saw us taking photographs. But he had the stuff on him.'

Dorothy Brant stood looking for a long time at the large, untidy blimp-like man who was still chuckling with pleasure. Then she joined in.

'I trust,' observed Dennis Jameson politely, 'that

everybody is having a good time. For myself, I've had a couple of unpleasant shocks today; and just for a moment I was afraid I should have another one. For a moment I honestly thought you were going to pitch on Mr Brant.'

'So did I,' agreed Dorothy, and beamed at her father. 'That's why it's so funny now.'

John Brant looked startled. But not half so startled as Colonel March.

'Now there,' the Colonel said, 'I honestly do not understand you. I am the Department of Queer Complaints. If you have a ghost in your attic or a foot print on top of your hedge, ring me up. But a certain success has blessed us because, as Mr Jameson says, I look for the obvious. And Lord love us! – if you have decided that a crime was committed by a gentleman who could walk on his hands, I will hold under torture that you are not likely to succeed by suspecting the one person in the house who has a crippled arm.'

A Wife in a Million

Val McDermid

The woman strolled through the supermarket, choosing a few items for her basket. As she reached the display of sauces and pickles, a muscle in her jaw tightened. She looked around, willing herself to appear casual. No one watched. Swiftly she took a jar of tomato pickle from her large leather handbag and placed it on the shelf. She moved on to the frozen meat section.

A few minutes later, she passed down the same aisle and paused. She repeated the exercise, this time adding two more jars to the shelf. As she walked on to the checkout, she felt tension slide from her body, leaving her light-headed.

She stood in the queue, anonymous among the morning shoppers, another neat woman in a well-cut winter coat, a faint smile on her face and a strangely unfocused look in her pale blue eyes.

Sarah Graham was sprawled on the sofa reading the Situations Vacant in the *Burnalder Evening News* when she heard the car pull up the drive. Sighing, she dropped the paper and went through to the kitchen. By the time she had pulled the cork from a bottle of elderflower wine and poured two glasses, the front door had opened and closed. Sarah stood, glasses in hand, facing the kitchen door.

Detective Sergeant Maggie Staniforth came into the kitchen, took the proffered glass and kissed Sarah perfunctorily. She walked into the living-room and slumped in a chair, calling over her shoulder, 'And what kind of day have you had?'

Sarah followed her through and shrugged. 'Another shitty day in paradise. You don't want to hear my catalogue of boredom.'

'You never bore me. And besides, it does me good to be reminded that there's a life outside crime.'

'I got up about nine, by which time you'd probably arrested half a dozen villains. I whizzed through the *Guardian* job ads, and went down the library to check out the other papers. After lunch I cleaned the bedroom, did a bit of ironing and polished the dining-room furniture. Then down to the newsagent's for the evening paper. A thrill a minute. And you? Solved the crime of the century?'

Maggie winced. 'Nothing so exciting. Bit of breaking and entering, bit of paperwork on the rape case at the blues club. It's due in court next week.'

'At least you get paid for it.'

'Something will come up soon, love.'

'And meanwhile I go on being your kept woman.'

Maggie said nothing. There was nothing to say. The two of them had been together since they fell head over heels in love at university eleven years before. Things had been fine while they were both concentrating on climbing their career ladders. But Sarah's career in personnel management had hit a brick wall when the company that employed her had collapsed nine months previously. That crisis had opened a wound in their relationship that was rapidly festering. Now Maggie was often afraid to speak for fear of provoking another bitter exchange. She drank her wine in silence.

'No titbits to amuse me, then?' Sarah demanded. 'No funny little tales from the underbelly?'

'One that might interest you,' Maggie said tentatively. 'Notice a story in the *News* last night about a woman taken to the General with suspected food poisoning?'

'I saw it. I read every inch of that paper. It fills an hour.'

'Well, she's died. The news came in just as I was leaving.

And there have apparently been another two families affected. The funny thing is that there doesn't seem to be a common source. Jim Bryant from casualty was telling me about it.'

Sarah pulled a face. 'Sure you can face my spaghetti carbonara tonight?'

The telephone cut across Maggie's smile. She quickly crossed the room and picked it up on the third ring. 'DS Staniforth speaking … Hi, Bill.' She listened intently. 'Good God!' she exclaimed. 'I'll be with you in ten minutes. OK?' She stood holding the phone. 'Sarah … that woman we were just talking about. It wasn't food poisoning. It was a massive dose of arsenic and two of the other so-called food poisoning cases have died. They suspect arsenic there too. I've got to go and meet Bill at the hospital.'

'You'd better get a move on, then. Shall I save you some food?'

'No point. And don't wait up, I'll be late.' Maggie crossed to Sarah and gave her a brief hug. She hurried out of the room. Seconds later, the front door slammed.

The fluorescent strips made the kitchen look bright but cold. The woman opened one of the fitted cupboards and took a jar of greyish-white powder from the very back of the shelf. She picked up a filleting knife whose edge was honed to a wicked sharpness. She slid it delicately under the flap of a cardboard pack of blancmange powder. She did the same to five other packets. Then she carefully opened the inner paper envelopes. Into each she mixed a tablespoonful of the powder from the jar.

Under the light, the grey strands in her auburn hair glinted. Painstakingly, she folded the inner packets closed again and with a drop of glue she resealed the cardboard packages. She put them all in a shopping bag and carried it into the rear porch.

She replaced the jar in the cupboard and went through to the living-room where the television blared. She looked strangely triumphant.

It was after three when Maggie Staniforth closed the front door behind her. As she hung up her sheepskin, she noticed lines of strain round her eyes in the hall mirror. Sarah appeared in the kitchen doorway. 'I know you're probably too tired to feel hungry, but I've made some soup if you want it,' she said.

'You shouldn't have stayed up. It's late.'

'I've got nothing else to do. After all, there's plenty of opportunity for me to catch up on my sleep.'

Please God, not now, thought Maggie. As if the job isn't hard enough without coming home to hassles from Sarah.

But she was proved wrong. Sarah smiled and said, 'So do you want some grub?'

'That depends.'

'On what?'

'Whether there's Higham's Continental Tomato Pickle in it.' Sarah looked bewildered. Maggie went on. 'It seems that three people have died from arsenic administered in Higham's Continental Tomato Pickle bought from Fastfare Supermarket.'

'You're joking!'

'Wish I was.' Maggie went through to the kitchen. She poured herself a glass of orange juice as Sarah served up a steaming bowl of lentil soup with a pile of buttered brown bread. Maggie sat down and tucked in, giving her lover a disjointed summary as she ate.

'Victim number one: May Scott, fifty-seven, widow, lived up Warburton Road. Numbers two and three: Gary Andrews, fifteen, and his brother Kevin, thirteen, from Priory Farm Estate. Their father is seriously ill. So are two others now, Thomas and Louise Foster of Bryony Grange. No connection between them except that they all ate pickle from jars bought on the same day at Fastfare.

'Could be someone playing at extortion – you know, pay me a million pounds or I'll do it again. Could be someone with a grudge against Fastfare. Ditto against Higham's. So you can bet your sweet life we're going to be hammered into the ground on this one. Already we're getting flak.'

Maggie finished her meal. Her head dropped into her hands. 'What a bitch of a job.'

'Better than no job at all.'

'Is it?'

'You should know better than to ask.'

Maggie sighed. 'Take me to bed, Sarah. Let me forget about the battlefield for a few hours, eh?'

Piped music lulled the shoppers at Pinkerton's Hypermarket into a drugged acquisitiveness. The woman pushing the trolley was deaf to its bland presence and its blandishments. When she reached the shelf with the instant desserts on display, she stopped and checked that the coast was clear.

She swiftly put three packs of blancmange on the shelf with their fellows and moved away. A few minutes later she returned and studied several cake mixes as she waited for the aisle to clear. Then she completed her mission and finished her shopping in a leisurely fashion.

At the checkout she chatted brightly to the bored teenager who rang up her purchases automatically. Then she left, gently humming the song that flowed from the shop's speakers.

Three days later, Maggie Staniforth burst into her

living-room in the middle of the afternoon to find Sarah
typing a job application. 'Red alert, love,' she announced.
'I'm only home to have a quick bath and change my things.
Any chance of a sandwich?'

'I was beginning to wonder if you still lived here,'
Sarah muttered darkly. 'If you were having an affair, at
least I'd know how to fight back.'

'Not now, love, please.'

'Do you want something hot? Soup? Omelette?'

'Soup, please. And a toasted cheese sandwich?'

'Coming up. What's the panic this time?'

Maggie's eyes clouded. 'Our homicidal maniac
has struck again. Eight people on the critical list at the
General. This time the arsenic was in Garratt's Blancmange from Pinkerton's Hypermarket. Bill's doing a television appeal right now asking for people to bring in any
packets bought there this week.'

'Different manufacturer, different supermarket. Sounds
like a crazy rather than a grudge, doesn't it?'

'And that makes the next strike impossible to predict.
Anyway, I'm going for that bath now. I'll be down again in
fifteen minutes.' Maggie stopped in the kitchen doorway,
'I'm not being funny, Sarah. Don't do any shopping in the
supermarkets. Butchers, greengrocers, okay. But no self-
service, pre-packaged food. Please.'

Sarah nodded. She had never seen Maggie afraid in

eight years in the force, and the sight did nothing to lift her depressed spirits.

This time it was jars of mincemeat. Even the Salvation Army band playing carols outside the Nationwide Stores failed to make the woman pause in her mission. Her shopping bag held six jars laced with deadly white powder when she entered the supermarket.

When she left, there were none. She dropped 50p in the collecting tin as she passed the band because they were playing her favourite carol, 'In the Bleak Midwinter'. She walked slowly back to the car park, not pausing to look at the shop-window Christmas displays. She wasn't anticipating a merry Christmas.

Sarah walked back from the newsagent's with the evening paper, reading the front page as she went. The Burnalder Poisoner was front-page news everywhere by now, but the stories in the local paper seemed to carry an extra edge of fear. They were thorough in their coverage, tracing any possible commercial connection between the three giant food companies that produced the contaminated food. They also speculated on the possible reasons for the week-long gaps between outbreaks. They laid out in stark detail the drastic effect the poisoning was having on the finances of the food-processing companies. And they noted the paradox of public hysteria about the poisoning while people still filled their shopping trolleys in anticipation of the festive season.

The latest killer was Univex mincemeat. Sarah shivered as she read of the latest three deaths, bringing the toll to twelve. As she turned the corner, she saw Maggie's car in the drive and increased her pace. A grim idea had taken root in her brain as she read the long report.

While she was hanging up her jacket, Maggie called from the kitchen. Sarah walked slowly through to find her tucking into a plate of eggs and bacon, but without her usual large dollop of tomato ketchup. There were dark circles beneath her eyes and the skin around them was grey and stretched. She had not slept at home for two nights. The job had never made such demands on her before. Sarah found a moment to wonder if the atmosphere between them was partly responsible for Maggie's total commitment to this desperate search.

'How is it going?' she asked anxiously.

'It's not,' said Maggie. 'Virtually nothing to go on. No link that we can find. It's not as if we even have proper leads to chase up. I came home for a break because we were just sitting staring at each other, wondering what to do next. Short of searching everyone who goes into the supermarkets, what can we do? And those bloody reporters seem to have taken up residence in the station. We're being leaned on from all sides. We've got to crack this soon or we'll be crucified.'

Sarah sat down. 'I've been giving this some thought. The grudge theory has broken down because you can't find a link between the companies, am I right?'

'Yes.'

'Have you thought about the effect unemployment has on crime?'

'Burglary, shoplifting, mugging, vandalism, drugs, yes. But surely not mass poisoning, love.'

'There's so much bitterness there, Maggie. So much hatred. I've often felt like murdering those incompetent tossers who destroyed Liddell's and threw me on the scrap-heap. Did you think about people who've been given the boot?'

'We did think about it. But only a handful of people have worked for all three companies. None of them have any reason to hold a grudge. And none of them have any connection with Burnalder.'

'There's another aspect, though, Maggie. It only hit me when I read the paper tonight. The *News* has a big piece about the parent companies who make the three products. Now, I'd swear that each one of those companies has advertised in the last couple of months for management executives. I know, I applied for two of the jobs. I didn't even get interviewed because I've got no experience in the food industry, only in plastics. There must be other people in the same boat, maybe less stable than I am.'

'My God!' Maggie breathed. She pushed her plate away.

The colour had returned to her cheeks and she seemed to have found fresh energy. She got up and hugged Sarah fiercely. 'You've given us the first positive lead in this whole bloody case. You're a genius!'

'I hope you'll remember that when they give you your inspector's job.'

Maggie grinned on her way out the door. 'I owe you one. I'll see you later.'

As the front door slammed, Sarah said ironically, 'I hope it's not too late already, babe.'

Detective Inspector Bill Nicholson had worked with Maggie Staniforth for two years. His initial distrust of her gender had been broken down by her sheer grasp of the job. Now he was wont to describe her as 'a bloody good copper in spite of being a woman', as if this were a discovery uniquely his, and a direct product of working for him. As she unfolded Sarah's suggestion, backed by photostats of newspaper advertisements culled from the local paper's files, he realised for the first time she was probably going to leapfrog him on the career ladder before too long. He didn't like the idea, but he wasn't prepared to let that stand between him and a job of work.

They started on the long haul of speaking directly to the personnel officers of the three companies. It meant quartering the country and they knew they were working against the clock. Back in Burnalder, a team of detectives was phoning companies who had advertised similar vacancies, asking for lists of applicants. The lumbering machinery of the law was in gear.

On the evening of the second day, an exhausted Maggie arrived home. Six hundred and thirty-seven miles of driving had taken their toll and she looked crumpled and older by ten years. Sarah helped her out of her coat and poured her a stiff drink in silence.

'You were right,' Maggie sighed. 'We've got the name and address of a man who has been rejected by all three firms after the first interview. We're moving in on him tonight. If he sticks to his pattern, he'll be aiming to strike again tomorrow. So with luck, it'll be a red-handed job.' She sounded grim and distant. 'What a bloody waste. Twelve lives because he can't get a bloody job.'

'I can understand it,' Sarah said abruptly and went through to the kitchen.

Maggie stared after her, shocked but comprehending. She felt again the low rumble of anger inside her against a system that set her to catch the people it had so often made its victims. If only Sarah had not lost her well-paid job, then Maggie knew she would have left the force by now, but they needed her salary to keep their heads above water. The job itself was dirty enough; but the added pain of keeping her relationship with Sarah constantly under wraps was gradually becoming more than she could comfortably bear. Sarah wasn't the only one whose choices had been drastically pruned by her unemployment.

By nine fifty-five a dozen detectives were stationed around a neat detached house in a quiet suburban street. In the garden a 'For Sale' sign sprouted among the rose bushes. Lights burned in the kitchen and living-room.

In the car, Bill made a final check of the search warrant. Then, after a last word over the radio, he and Maggie walked up the short drive.

'It's up to you now,' he said and rang the doorbell. It was answered by a tall, bluff man in his mid-forties. There were lines of strain round his eyes and his clothes hung loosely, as if he had recently lost weight.

'Yes?' he asked in a pleasant, gentle voice.

'Mr Derek Millfield?' Maggie demanded.

'That's me. How can I help you?'

'We're police officers, Mr Millfield. We'd like to have a word with you, if you don't mind.'

He looked puzzled. 'By all means. But I don't see what...' His voice tailed off. 'You'd better come in, I suppose.'

They entered the house and Millfield showed them into a surprisingly large living-room. It was tastefully and expensively furnished. A woman sat watching television.

'My wife Shula,' he explained. 'Shula, these are police-men – I mean officers. Sorry, miss.'

Shula Millfield stood up and faced them. 'You've come for me, then,' she said.

It was hard to say who looked most surprised. Then suddenly she was laughing, crying and screaming, all at once.

Maggie stretched out on the sofa. 'It was appalling. She must have been living on a knife-edge for weeks before she finally flipped. He's been out of work for seven months. They've had to take their kids out of private school, had to sell a car, sell their possessions. He had no idea what she was up to. I've never seen anyone go berserk like that. All for the sake of a nice middle-class lifestyle.

'There's no doubt about her guilt, either. Her finger-prints are all over the jar of arsenic. She stole the jar a month ago. She worked part-time in the pharmacy at the cottage hospital in Kingcaple. But they didn't notice the loss. God knows how. Deputy-heads will roll,' she added bitterly.

'What will happen to her?' Sarah asked coolly.

'She'll be tried, if she's fit to plead. But I doubt if she will be. I'm afraid it'll be the locked ward for life.' When she looked up, Maggie saw there were tears on Sarah's cheeks. She immediately got up and put an arm round her. 'Hey, don't cry, love. Please.'

'I can't help it, Maggie. You see, I know how she feels. I know that utter lack of all hope. I know that hatred, that sense of frustration and futility. There's nothing you can do to take that away. What you have to live with, Detective-Sergeant Staniforth, is that it could have been me.

'It could so easily have been me.'

The Dagger with Wings

G. K. Chesterton

Father Brown, at one period of his life, found it difficult to hang his hat on a hat-peg without repressing a slight shudder. The origin of this idiosyncrasy was indeed a mere detail in much more complicated events; but it was perhaps the only detail that remained to him in his busy life to remind him of the whole business. Its remote origin was to be found in the facts which led Dr Boyne, the medical officer attached to the police force, to send for the priest on a particular frosty morning in December.

Dr Boyne was a big dark Irishman, one of those rather baffling Irishmen to be found all over the world, who will talk scientific scepticism, materialism and cynicism at length and at large, but who never dream of referring anything touching the ritual of religion to anything except the traditional religion of their native land. It would be hard to say whether their creed is a very superficial varnish or a very fundamental substratum; but most probably it is both, with a mass of materialism in between. Anyhow, when he thought that matters of that sort might be involved, he asked Father Brown to call, though he made no pretence of preference for that aspect of them.

'I'm not sure I want you, you know,' was his greeting. 'I'm not sure about anything yet. I'm hanged if I can make out whether it's a case for a doctor, or a policeman, or a priest.'

'Well,' said Father Brown with a smile, 'as I suppose you're both a policeman and a doctor, I seem to be rather in a minority.'

'I admit you're what politicians call an instructed minority,' replied the doctor. 'I mean, I know you've had to do a little in our line as well as your own. But it's precious hard to say whether this business is in your line or ours, or merely in the line of the Commissioners in Lunacy. We've just had a message from a man living near here, in that white house on the hill, asking for protection against a murderous persecution. We've gone into the facts as far as we could, and perhaps I'd better tell you the story, as it is supposed to have happened, from the beginning.

'It seems that a man named Aylmer, who was a wealthy landowner in the West Country, married rather late in life

and had three sons, Philip, Stephen and Arnold. But in his
bachelor days, when he thought he would have no heir, he
had adopted a boy whom he thought very brilliant and
promising, who went by the name of John Strake. His
origin seems to be vague; they say he was a foundling;
some say he was a gipsy. I think the last notion is mixed up
with the fact that Aylmer in his old age dabbled in all sorts
of dingy occultism, including palmistry and astrology,
and his three sons say that Strake encouraged him in it.
But they said a great many other things besides that. They
said Strake was an amazing scoundrel, and especially an
amazing liar; a genius in inventing lies on the spur of the
moment, and telling them so as to deceive a detective. But
that might very well be a natural prejudice, in the light of
what happened. Perhaps you can more or less imagine
what happened. The old man left practically everything
to the adopted son; and when he died the three real sons
disputed the will. They said their father had been frightened into surrender and, not to put too fine a point on it,
into gibbering idiocy. They said Strake had the strangest
and most cunning ways of getting at him, in spite of the
nurses and the family, and terrorizing him on his death-
bed. Anyhow, they seemed to have proved something
about the dead man's mental condition, for the courts set
aside the will and the sons inherited. Strake is said to have
broken out in the most dreadful fashion, and sworn he

would kill all three of them, one after another, and that nothing could hide them from his vengeance. It is the third or last of the brothers, Arnold Aylmer, who is asking for police protection.'

'Third and last,' said the priest, looking at him gravely.

'Yes,' said Boyne. 'The other two are dead.'

There was a silence before he continued. 'That is where the doubt comes in. There is no proof they were murdered, but they might possibly have been. The eldest, who took up his position as squire, was supposed to have committed suicide in his garden. The second, who went into trade as a manufacturer, was knocked on the head by the machinery in his factory; he might very well have taken a false step and fallen. But if Strake did kill them, he is certainly very cunning in his way of getting to work and getting away. On the other hand, it's more than likely that the whole thing is a mania of conspiracy founded on a coincidence. Look here, what I want is this. I want somebody of sense, who isn't an official, to go up and have a talk to this Mr Arnold Aylmer, and form an impression of him. You know what a man with a delusion is like, and how a man looks when he is telling the truth. I want you to be the advance guard, before we take the matter up.'

'It seems rather odd,' said Father Brown, 'that you haven't had to take it up before. If there is anything in this business, it seems to have been going on for a good time. Is there any particular reason why he should send for you just now, any more than any other time?'

'That had occurred to me, as you may imagine,' answered Dr Boyne. 'He does give a reason, but I confess it is one of the things that make me wonder whether the whole thing isn't only the whim of some half-witted crank. He declared that all his servants have suddenly gone on strike and left him, so that he is obliged to call on the police to look after his house. And on making inquiries, I certainly do find that there has been a general exodus of servants from that house on the hill; and of course the town is full of tales, very one-sided tales I dare say. Their account of it seems to be that their employer had become quite impossible in his fidgets and fears and exactions; that he wanted them to guard the house like sentries, or sit up like night nurses in a hospital; that they could never be left alone because he must never be left alone. So they all announced in a loud voice that he was a lunatic, and left. Of course that does not prove he is a lunatic; but it seems rather rum nowadays for a man to expect his valet or his parlourmaid to act as an armed guard.'

'And so,' said the priest with a smile, 'he wants a policeman to act as his parlourmaid because his parlourmaid won't act as a policeman.'

'I thought that rather thick, too,' agreed the doctor; but

I can't take the responsibility of a flat refusal till I've tried a compromise. You are the compromise.'

'Very well,' said Father Brown simply. 'I'll go and call on him now if you like.'

The rolling country round the little town was sealed and bound with frost, and the sky was as clear and cold as steel, except in the north-east where clouds with lurid haloes were beginning to climb up the sky. It was against these darker and more sinister colours that the house on the hill gleamed with a row of pale pillars, forming a short colonnade of the classical sort. A winding road led up to it across the curve of the down and plunged into a mass of dark bushes. Just before it reached the bushes the air seemed to grow colder and colder, as if he were approaching an ice-house or the North Pole. But he was a highly practical person, never entertaining such fancies except as fancies. And he merely cocked his eye at the great livid cloud crawling up over the house, and remarked cheerfully:

'It's going to snow.'

Through a low ornamental iron gateway of the Italianate pattern he entered a garden having something of that desolation which only belongs to the disorder of orderly things. Deep-green growths were grey with the faint powder of the frost, large weeds had fringed the fading pattern of the flower-beds as if in a ragged frame;

and the house stood as if waist-high in a stunted forest of shrubs and bushes. The vegetation consisted largely of evergreens or very hardy plants; and though it was thus thick and heavy, it was too northern to be called luxuriant. It might be described as an Arctic jungle. So it was in some sense with the house itself, which had a row of columns and a classical facade, which might have looked out on the Mediterranean; but which seemed now to be withering in the wind of the North Sea. Classical ornament here and there accentuated the contrast; caryatides and carved masks of comedy or tragedy looked down from corners of the building upon the grey confusion of the garden paths; but the faces seemed to be frost-bitten. The very volutes of the capitals might have curled up with the cold.

Father Brown went up the grassy steps to a square porch flanked by big pillars and knocked at the door. About four minutes afterwards he knocked again. Then he stood still patiently waiting with his back to the door and looked out on the slowly darkening landscape. It was darkening under the shadow of that one great continent of cloud that had come flying out of the north; and even as he looked out beyond the pillars of the porch, which seemed huge and black above him in the twilight, he saw the opalescent crawling rim of the great cloud as it sailed over the roof and bowed over the porch like a canopy. The grey canopy with its faintly coloured fringes seemed to sink lower and lower upon the garden beyond, until what had recently been a clear and pale-hued winter sky was left in a few silver ribbons and rags like a sickly sunset. Father Brown waited, and there was no sound within.

Then he betook himself briskly down the steps and round the house to look for another entrance. He eventually found one, a side door in the flat wall, and on this also he hammered and outside this also he waited. Then he tried the handle and found the door apparently bolted or fastened in some fashion; and then he moved along that side of the house, musing on the possibilities of the position, and wondering whether the eccentric Mr Aylmer had barricaded himself too deep in the house to hear any kind of summons; or whether perhaps he would barricade himself all the more, on the assumption that any summons must be the challenge of the avenging Strake. It might be that the decamping servants had only unlocked one door when they left in the morning, and that their master had locked that; but whatever he might have done it was unlikely that they, in the mood of that moment, had looked so carefully to the defences. He continued his prowl round the place; it was not really a large place, though perhaps a little pretentious; and in a few moments he found he had made the complete circuit. A moment after he found what he suspected and sought. The french window of one room, curtained and shadowed with creeper, stood open by a crack, doubtless accidentally left ajar, and he found himself in a central room, comfortably upholstered in a rather old-fashioned way, with a staircase leading up from it on one side and a door leading out of it on the other. Immediately opposite him was another door with red glass let into it, a little gaudily for later tastes; something that looked like a red-robed figure in cheap stained glass. On a round table to the right stood a sort of aquarium – a great bowl full of greenish water, in which fishes and similar things moved about as in a tank; and just opposite it a plant of the palm variety with very large green leaves. All this looked so very dusty and Early Victorian that the telephone, visible in the curtained alcove, was almost a surprise.

'Who is that?' a voice called out sharply and rather suspiciously from behind the stained-glass door.

'Could I see Mr Aylmer?' asked the priest apologetically.

The door opened and a gentleman in a peacock-green dressing-gown came out with an inquiring look. His hair was rather rough and untidy, as if he had been in bed or lived in a state of slowly getting up, but his eyes were not only awake but alert, and some would have said alarmed. Father Brown knew that the contradiction was likely enough in a man who had rather run to seed under the shadow either of a delusion or a danger. He had a fine aquiline face when seen in profile, but when seen full face the first impression was of the untidiness and even the wilderness of his loose brown beard.

'I am Mr Aylmer,' he said, 'but I have got out of the way of expecting visitors.'

Something about Mr Aylmer's unrestful eye prompted the priest to go straight to the point. If the man's persecution was only a monomania, he would be the less likely to resent it.

'I was wondering,' said Father Brown softly, 'whether it is quite true that you never expect visitors.'

'You are right,' replied his host steadily. 'I always expect one visitor. And he may be the last.'

'I hope not,' said Father Brown, 'but at least I am relieved to infer that I do not look very like him.'

Mr Aylmer shook himself with a sort of savage laugh. 'You certainly do not,' he said.

'Mr Aylmer,' said Father Brown frankly, 'I apologize for the liberty, but some friends of mine have told me about your trouble, and asked me to see if I could do anything for you. The truth is, I have some little experience in affairs like this.'

'There are no affairs like this,' said Aylmer.

'You mean,' observed Father Brown, 'that the tragedies in your unfortunate family were not normal deaths?'

'I mean they were not even normal murders,' answered the other. 'The man who is hounding us all to death is a hell-hound, and his power is from hell.'

'All evil has one origin,' said the priest gravely. 'But how do you know they were not normal murders?'

Aylmer answered with a gesture which offered his guest a chair; then he seated himself slowly in another, frowning, with his hands on his knees; but when he looked up his expression had grown milder and more thoughtful, and his voice was quite cordial and composed.

'Sir,' he said, 'I don't want you to imagine that I'm in the least an unreasonable person. I have come to these conclusions by reason, because unfortunately reason really leads there. I have read a great deal on these subjects; for I was the only one who inherited my father's scholarship in somewhat obscure matters, and I have since inherited his library. But what I tell you does not rest on what I have read but on what I have seen.'

Father Brown nodded, and the other proceeded, as if picking his words:

'In my elder brother's case I was not certain at first. There were no marks or footprints where he was found shot, and the pistol was left beside him. But he had just received a threatening letter, certainly from our enemy, for it was marked with a sign like a winged dagger, which was one of his infernal cabalistic tricks. And a servant said she had seen something moving along the garden wall in the twilight that was much too large to be a cat. I leave it there; all I can say is that if the murderer came, he managed to leave no traces of his coming. But when my brother Stephen died it was different; and since then I have known. A machine was working in an open scaffolding under the factory tower; I scaled the platform a moment after he had fallen under the iron hammer that struck him; I did not see anything else strike him, but I saw what I saw.

'A great drift of factory smoke was rolling between me and the factory tower; but through a rift of it I saw on the top of it a dark human figure wrapped in what looked like a black cloak. Then the sulphurous smoke drove between us again; and when it cleared I looked up at the distant chimney – there was nobody there. I am a rational man, and I will ask all rational men how he had reached that dizzy unapproachable turret, and how he left it.

He stared across at the priest with a sphinx-like challenge; then after a silence he said abruptly:

'My brother's brains were knocked out, but his body was not much damaged. And in his pocket we found one of those warning messages dated the day before and stamped with the flying dagger.

'I am sure,' he went on gravely, 'that the symbol of the winged dagger is not merely arbitrary or accidental. Nothing about that abominable man is accidental. He is all design; though it is indeed a most dark and intricate design. His mind is woven not only out of elaborate schemes but out of all sorts of secret languages and signs, and dumb signals and wordless pictures which are the names of nameless things. He is the worst sort of man that the world knows: he is the wicked mystic. Now, I don't pretend to penetrate all that is conveyed by this symbol; but it seems surely that it must have a relation to all that was most remarkable, or even incredible, in his movements as he had hovered round my unfortunate family. Is there no connexion between the idea of a winged weapon and the mystery by which Philip was struck dead on his own lawn without the lightest touch of any footprint having disturbed the dust or grass? Is there no connexion between the plumed poignard flying like a feathered arrow and that figure which hung on the far top of the toppling chimney, clad in a cloak for pinions?'

'You mean,' said Father Brown thoughtfully, 'that he is in a perpetual state of levitation'.

'Simon Magus did it,' replied Aylmer, 'and it was one of the commonest predictions of the Dark Ages that Antichrist would be able to fly. Anyhow, there was the flying dagger on the document; and whether or no it could fly, it could certainly strike.'

'Did you notice what sort of paper it was on?' asked Father Brown. 'Common paper?'

The sphinx-like face broke abruptly into a harsh laugh.

'You can see what they're like,' said Aylmer grimly, 'for I got one myself this morning.'

He was leaning back in his chair now, with his long legs thrust out from under the green dressing-gown, which was a little short for him, and his bearded chin pillowed on his chest. Without moving otherwise, he thrust his hand deep in the dressing-gown pocket and held out a fluttering scrap of paper at the end of a rigid arm. His whole attitude was suggestive of a sort of paralysis, that was both rigidity and collapse. But the next remark of the priest had a curious effect of rousing him.

Father Brown was blinking in his short-sighted way at the paper presented to him. It was a singular sort of paper, rough without being common, as from an artist's sketch-book; and on it was drawn boldly in red ink a dagger decorated with wings like the rod of Hermes, with the written words, 'Death comes the day after this, as it came to your brothers.'

Father Brown tossed the paper on the floor and sat bolt upright in his chair.

'You mustn't let that sort of stuff stupefy you,' he said sharply. 'These devils always try to make us helpless by making us hopeless.'

Rather to his surprise, an awakening wave went over the prostrate figure, which sprang from its chair as if startled out of a dream.

'You're right, you're right!' cried Aylmer with a rather uncanny animation; 'and the devils shall find I'm not so hopeless after all, nor so helpless either. Perhaps I have more hope and better help than you fancy.'

He stood with his hands in his pockets, frowning down at the priest, who had a momentary doubt, during that strained silence, about whether the man's long peril had not touched his brain. But when he spoke it was quite soberly.

'I believe my unfortunate brothers failed because they used the wrong weapons. Philip carried a revolver, and that was how his death came to be called suicide. Stephen had police protection, but he also had a sense of what made him ridiculous; and he could not allow a policeman to climb up a ladder after him to a scaffolding where he stood only a moment. They were both scoffers, reacting into scepticism from the strange mysticism of my father's last days. But I always knew there was more in my father than they understood. It is true that by studying magic he fell at last under the blight of black magic; the black magic of this scoundrel Strake. But my brothers were wrong about the antidote. The antidote to black magic is not brute materialism or worldly wisdom. The antidote to black magic is white magic.'

'It rather depends,' said Father Brown, 'what you mean by white magic.'

'I mean silver magic,' said the other, in a low voice, like one speaking of a secret revelation. Then after a silence, he said: 'Do you know what I mean by silver magic? Excuse me a moment.'

He turned and opened the central door with the red glass and went into a passage beyond it. The house had less depth than Brown had supposed; instead of the door opening into interior rooms, the corridor it revealed ended in another door on the garden. The door of one room was on one side of the passage; doubtless, the priest told himself, the proprietor's bedroom whence he had rushed out in his dressing-gown. There was nothing else on that side but an ordinary hat-stand with the ordinary dingy cluster of old hats and overcoats; but on the other side was something more interesting: a very dark old oak sideboard laid out with some old silver, and overhung by a trophy or ornament of old weapons. It was by that that Arnold Aylmer halted, looking up at a long, antiquated pistol with a bell-shaped mouth.

The door at the end of the passage was barely open, and through the crack came a streak of white daylight. The priest had very quick instincts about natural things, and something in the unusual brilliancy of that white line told him what had happened outside. It was indeed what he had prophesied when he was approaching the house. He ran past his rather startled host and opened the door, to face something that was at once a blank and a blaze. What he had seen shining through the crack was not only the most negative whiteness of daylight but the positive whiteness of snow. All round, the sweeping fall of the country was covered with that shining pallor that seems at once hoary and innocent.

'Here is white magic anyhow,' said Father Brown in his cheerful voice. Then, as he turned back into the hall, he murmured, 'And silver magic too, I suppose,' for the white lustre touched the silver with splendour and lit up the old steel here and there in the darkling armoury. The shaggy head of the brooding Aylmer seemed to have a halo of silver fire, as he turned with his face in shadow and the outlandish pistol in his hand.

'Do you know why I choose this sort of old blunderbuss?' he asked. 'Because I can load it with this sort of bullet.'

He had picked up a small apostle spoon from the sideboard, and by sheer violence broke off the small figure at the top. 'Let us go back into the other room,' he added.

'Did you ever read about the death of Dundee?' he asked when they had reseated themselves. He had recovered from his momentary annoyance at the priest's restlessness. 'Graham of Claverhouse, you know, who persecuted the Covenanters and had a black horse that could ride straight up a precipice. Don't you know he could only be shot with a silver bullet, because he had sold himself to the Devil? That's one comfort about you; at least you know enough to believe in the Devil.'

'Oh, yes,' replied Father Brown, I believe in the Devil. What I don't believe in is the Dundee. I mean the Dundee of Covenanting legends, with his nightmare of a horse. John Graham was simply a seventeenth-century professional soldier, rather better than most. If he dragooned them it was because he was a dragoon, but not a dragon. Now my experience is that it's not that sort of swaggering blade who sells himself to the Devil. The devil-worshippers I've known were quite different. Not to mention names, which might cause a social flutter, I'll take a man in Dundee's own day. Have you ever heard of Dalrymple of Stair?'

'No,' replied the other gruffly.

'You've heard of what he did,' said Father Brown, 'and it was worse than anything Dundee ever did; yet he escapes the infamy by oblivion. He was the man who made the Massacre of Glencoe. He was a very learned man and lucid lawyer, a statesman with very serious and enlarged ideas of statesmanship, a quiet man with a very refined and intellectual face. That's the sort of man who sells himself to the Devil.'

Aylmer half started from his chair with an enthusiasm of eager assent.

'By God! you are right,' he cried. 'A refined intellectual face! That is the face of John Strake.'

Then he raised himself and stood looking at the priest with a curious concentration. 'If you will wait here a little while,' he said, 'I will show you something.'

He went back through the central door, closing it after him; going, the priest presumed, to the old side-board or possibly to his bedroom. Father Brown remained seated, gazing abstractedly at the carpet, where a faint red glimmer shone from the glass in the doorway. Once it seemed to brighten like a ruby and then darkened again, as if the sun of that stormy day had passed from cloud to cloud. Nothing moved except the aquatic creatures which floated to and fro in the dim green bowl. Father Brown was thinking hard.

A minute or two afterwards he got up and slipped quietly to the alcove of the telephone, where he rang up his friend Dr Boyne, at the official headquarters. 'I wanted to tell you about Aylmer and his affairs,' he said quietly. 'It's a queer story, but I rather think there's something in it. If I were you I'd send some men up here straight away; four or five men, I think, and surround the house. If anything does happen there'll probably be something startling in the way of an escape.'

Then he went back and sat down again, staring at the dark carpet, which again glowed blood-red with the light from the glass door. Something in that filtered light set his mind drifting on certain borderlands of thought, with the first white daybreak before the coming of colour, and all that mystery which is alternately veiled and revealed in the symbol of windows and of doors.

An inhuman howl in a human voice came from beyond the closed doors, almost simultaneously with the noise of firing. Before the echoes of the shot had died away the door was violently flung open and his host staggered into the room, the dressing-gown half torn from his shoulder and the long pistol smoking in his hand. He seemed to be shaking in every limb, yet he was shaken in part with an unnatural laughter.

'Glory be to the White Magic!' he cried; 'Glory be to the silver bullet! The hell-hound has hunted once too often, and my brothers are avenged at last.'

He sank into a chair and the pistol slid from his hand and fell on the floor. Father Brown darted past him, slipped through the glass door and went down the passage. As he did so he put his hand on the handle of the bedroom door, as if half intending to enter; then he stooped a moment, as if examining something – and then he ran to the outer door and opened it.

On the field of snow, which had been so blank a little while before, lay one black object. At the first glance it looked a little like an enormous bat. A second glance showed that it was, after all, a human figure; fallen on its face, the whole head covered by a broad black hat having something of a Latin-American look; while the appearance of black-wings came from the two flaps or loose sleeves of a very vast black cloak spread out, perhaps by accident, to their utmost length on either side. Both the hands were hidden, though Father Brown thought he could detect the position of one of them, and saw close to it, under the edge of the cloak, the glimmer of some metallic weapon. The main effect, however, was curiously like that of the simple extravagances of heraldry; like a black eagle displayed on a white ground. But by walking round it and peering under the hat the priest got a glimpse of the face, which was indeed what his host had called refined and intellectual; even sceptical and austere: the face of John Strake.

'Well, I'm jiggered,' muttered Father Brown. 'It really does look like some vast vampire that has swooped down like a bird.'

'How else could he have come?' came a voice from the doorway, and Father Brown looked up to see Aylmer once more standing there.

'Couldn't he have walked?' replied Father Brown evasively.

Aylmer stretched out his arm and swept the white landscape with a gesture.

'Look at the snow,' he said in a deep voice that had a sort of roll and thrill in it. 'Is not the snow unspotted

– pure as the white magic you yourself called it? Is there a speck on it for miles, save that one foul black blot that has fallen there? There are no footprints, but a few of yours and mine; there are none approaching the house from anywhere.'

Then he looked at the little priest for a moment with a concentrated and curious expression, and said:

'I will tell you something else. That cloak he flies with is too long to walk with. He was not a very tall man, and it would trail behind him like a royal train. Stretch it out over his body, if you like, and see.'

'What happened to you both?' asked Father Brown abruptly.

'It was too swift to describe,' answered Aylmer. 'I had looked out of the door and was turning back when there came a kind of rushing of wind all around me, as if I were being buffeted by a wheel revolving in mid-air. I spun round somehow and fired blindly; and then I saw nothing but what you see now. But I am morally certain you wouldn't see it if I had not had a silver shot in my gun. It would have been a different body lying there in the snow.'

'By the way,' remarked Father Brown, 'shall we leave it lying there in the snow? Or would you like it taken into your room – I suppose that's your bedroom in the passage?'

'No, no,' replied Aylmer hastily; 'we must leave it there till the police have seen it. Besides, I've had as much of such things as I can stand for the moment. Whatever else happens, I'm going to have a drink. After that, they can hang me if they like.'

Inside the central apartment, between the palm plant and the bowl of fishes, Aylmer tumbled into a chair. He had nearly knocked the bowl over as he lurched into the room, but he had managed to find the decanter of brandy after plunging his hand rather blindly into several cupboards and corners. He did not at any time look like a methodical person, but at this moment his distraction must have been extreme. He drank with a long gulp and began to talk rather feverishly, as if to fill up a silence.

'I see you are still doubtful,' he said, 'though you have seen the thing with your own eyes. Believe me, there was something more behind the quarrel between the spirit of Strake and the spirit of the house of Aylmer. Besides, you have no business to be an unbeliever. You ought to stand for all the things these stupid people call superstitions. Come now, don't you think there's a lot in those old wives' tales about luck and charms and so on, silver bullets included? What do you say about them as a Catholic?'

'I say I'm an agnostic,' replied Father Brown, smiling.

'Nonsense,' said Aylmer impatiently. 'It's your business to believe things.'

'Well, I do believe some things, of course,' conceded Father Brown; 'and therefore, of course, I don't believe other things.'

Aylmer was leaning forward, and looking at him with a strange intensity that was almost like that of a mesmerist.

'You do believe it,' he said. 'You do believe everything. We all believe everything, even when we deny everything. The deniers believe. The unbelievers believe. Don't you feel in your heart that these contradictions do not really contradict: that there is a cosmos that contains them all? The soul goes round upon a wheel of stars and all things return; perhaps Strake and I have striven in many shapes, beast against beast and bird against bird, and perhaps we shall strive for ever. But since we seek and need each other, even that eternal hatred is an eternal love. Good and evil go round in a wheel that is one thing and not many. Do you not realize in your heart, do you not believe behind all your beliefs, that there is but one reality and we are its shadows; and that all things are but aspects of one thing: a centre where men melt into Man and Man into God?'

'No,' said Father Brown.

Outside, twilight had begun to fall, in that phase of such a snow-laden evening when the land looks brighter than the sky. In the porch of the main entrance, visible through a half-curtained window, Father Brown could dimly see a bulky figure standing. He glanced casually at the french windows through which he had originally entered, and saw they were darkened with two equally motionless figures. The inner door with the coloured glass stood slightly ajar; and he could see in the short corridor beyond, the ends of two long shadows, exaggerated and distorted by the level light of evening, but still like grey caricatures of the figures of men. Dr Boyne had already obeyed his telephone message. The house was surrounded.

'What is the good of saying no?' insisted his host, still with the same hypnotic stare. 'You have seen part of that eternal drama with your own eyes. You have seen the threat of John Strake to slay Arnold Aylmer by black magic. You have seen Arnold Aylmer slay John Strake by white magic. You see Arnold Aylmer alive and talking to you now. And yet you do not believe it.'

'No, I do not believe it,' said Father Brown, and rose from his chair like one terminating a visit.

'Why not?' asked the other.

The priest only lifted his voice a little, but it sounded in every corner of the room like a bell.

'Because you are not Arnold Aylmer,' he said. 'I know who you are. Your name is John Strake; and you have murdered the last of the brothers, who is lying outside in the snow.'

A ring of white showed round the iris of the other

man's eyes; he seemed to be making, with bursting eye-balls, a last effort to mesmerize and master his companion. Then he made a sudden movement sideways; and even as he did so the door behind him opened and a big detective in plain clothes put one hand quietly on his shoulder. The other hand hung down, but it held a revolver. The man looked wildly round, and saw plainclothes men in all corners of the quiet room.

That evening Father Brown had another and longer conversation with Dr Boyne about the tragedy of the Aylmer family. By that time there was no longer any doubt of the central fact of the case, for John Strake had confessed his identity and even confessed his crimes; only it would be truer to say that he boasted of his victories. Compared to the fact that he had rounded off his life's work with the last Aylmer lying dead, everything else, including existence itself, seemed to be indifferent to him.

'The man is a sort of monomaniac,' said Father Brown. 'He is not interested in any other matter; not even in any other murder. I owe him something for that; for I had to comfort myself with the reflection a good many times this afternoon. As has doubtless occurred to you, instead of weaving all that wild but ingenious romance about winged vampires and silver bullets, he might have put an ordinary leaden bullet into me, and walked out of the house. I assure you it occurred quite frequently to me.'

'I wonder why he didn't,' observed Boyne. 'I don't understand it; but I don't understand anything yet. How on earth did you discover it, and what in the world did you discover?'

'Oh, you provided me with very valuable information,' replied Father Brown modestly, 'especially the one piece of information that really counted. I mean the statement that Strake was a very inventive and imaginative liar, with great presence of mind in producing his lies. This afternoon he needed it; but he rose to the occasion. Perhaps his only mistake was in choosing a preternatural story; he had the notion that because I am a clergyman I should believe anything. Many people have little notions of that kind.'

'But I can't make head or tail of it,' said the doctor. 'You must really begin at the beginning.'

'The beginning of it was a dressing-gown,' said Father Brown simply. 'It was the one really good disguise I've ever known. When you meet a man in a house with a dressing-gown on, you assume quite automatically that he's in his own house. I assumed it myself; but afterwards queer little things began to happen. When he took the pistol down he clicked it at arm's length, as a man does to make sure a strange weapon isn't loaded; of course he would know whether the pistols in his own hall were loaded or not. I didn't like the way he looked for the brandy, or the way he nearly barged into the bowl of fishes. For a man who has a fragile thing of that sort as a fixture in his rooms gets a quite mechanical habit of avoiding it. But these things might possibly have been fancies; the first real point was this. He came out from the little passage between the two doors; and in that passage there's only one other door leading to a room; so I assumed it was the bedroom he had just come from. I tried the handle; but it was locked. I thought this odd; and looked through the keyhole. It was an utterly bare room, obviously deserted; no bed, no anything. Therefore he had not come from inside any room, but from outside the house. And when I saw that, I think I saw the whole picture.

'Poor Arnold Aylmer doubtless slept and perhaps lived upstairs, and came down in his dressing-gown and passed through the red glass door. At the end of the passage, black against the winter daylight, he saw the enemy of his house. He saw a tall bearded man in a broad-brimmed black hat and a large flapping black cloak. He did not see much more in this world. Strake sprang on him, throttling or stabbing him; we cannot be sure till the inquest. Then Strake, standing in the narrow passage between the hat-stand and the old sideboard, and looking down in triumph on the last of his foes, heard something he had not expected. He heard footsteps in the parlour beyond. It was myself entering by the french windows.

'His masquerade was a miracle of promptitude. It

involved not only a disguise but a romance – an impromptu romance. He took off his big black hat and cloak and put on the dead man's dressing-gown. Then he did a rather grisly thing; at least a thing that affects my fancy as more grisly than the rest. He hung the corpse like a coat on one of the hatpegs. He draped it in his own long cloak, and found it hung well below the heels; he covered the head entirely with his own wide hat. It was the only possible way of hiding it in that little passage with the locked door; but it was really a very clever one. I myself walked past the hat-stand once without knowing it was anything but a hat-stand. I think that unconsciousness of mine will always give me a shiver.

'He might perhaps have left it at that; but I might have discovered the corpse at any minute; and, hung where it was, it was a corpse calling for what you might call an explanation. He adopted the bolder stroke of discovering it himself and explaining it himself.

'Then there dawned on this strange and frightfully fertile mind the conception of a story of substitution; the reversal of the parts. He had already assumed the part of Arnold Aylmer. Why should not his dead enemy assume the part of John Strake? There must have been something in that topsy-turvydom to take the fancy of that darkly fanciful man. It was like some frightful fancy-dress ball to which the two mortal enemies were to go dressed up as each other. Only, the fancy-dress ball was to be a dance of death: and one of the dancers would be dead. That is why I can imagine that man putting it in his own mind, and I can imagine him smiling.'

Father Brown was gazing into vacancy with his large grey eyes, which, when not blurred by his trick of blinking, were the one notable thing in his face. He went on speaking simply and seriously:

'All things are from God; and above all, reason and imagination and the great gifts of the mind. They are good in themselves; and we must not altogether forget their origin even in their perversion. Now this man had in him a very noble power to be perverted; the power of telling stories. He was a great novelist; only he had twisted his fictive power to practical and to evil ends; to deceiving men with false fact instead of with true fiction. It began with his deceiving old Aylmer with elaborate excuses and ingeniously detailed lies; but even that may have been, at the beginning, little more than the tall stories and tarradiddles of the child who may say equally he has seen the King of England or the King of the Fairies. It grew strong in him through the vice that perpetuates all vices, pride; he grew more and more vain of his promptitude in producing stories of his originality, and subtlety in developing them. That is what the young Aylmers meant by saying that he could always cast a spell over their father;

and it was true. It was the sort of spell that the story-teller cast over the tyrant in the Arabian Nights. And to the last he walked the world with the pride of a poet, and with the false yet unfathomable courage of a great liar. He could always produce more Arabian Nights if ever his neck was in danger. And today his neck was in danger.

'But I am sure, as I say, that he enjoyed it as a fantasy as well as a conspiracy. He set about the task of telling the true story the wrong way round: of treating the dead man as living and the live man as dead. He had already got into Aylmer's dressing-gown; he proceeded to get into Aylmer's body and soul. He looked at the corpse as if it were his own corpse lying cold in the snow. Then he spread-eagled it in that strange fashion to suggest the sweeping descent of a bird of prey, and decked it out not only in his own dark and flying garments but in a whole dark fairy-tale about the black bird that could only fall by the silver bullet. I do not know whether it was the silver glittering on the sideboard or the snow shining beyond the door that suggested to his intensely artistic temperament the theme of white magic and the white metal used against magicians. But whatever its origin, he made it his own like a poet; and did it very promptly, like a practical man. He completed the exchange and reversal of parts by flinging the corpse out on to the snow as the corpse of Strake. He did his best to work up a creepy conception of

Strake as something hovering in the air everywhere, a harpy with wings of speed and claws of death; to explain the absence of foot-prints and other things. For one piece of artistic impudence I hugely admire him. He actually turned one of the contradictions in his case into an argument for it; and said that the man's cloak being too long for him proved that he never walked on the ground like an ordinary mortal. But he looked at me very hard while he said that; and something told me that he was at that moment trying a very big bluff.'

Dr Boyne looked thoughtful. 'Had you discovered the truth by then?' he asked. 'There is something very queer and close to the nerves, I think, about notions affecting identity. I don't know whether it would be more weird to get a guess like that swiftly or slowly. I wonder when you suspected and when you were sure.'

'I think I really suspected when I telephoned to you,' replied his friend. 'And it was nothing more than the red light from the closed door brightening and darkening on the carpet. It looked like a splash of blood that grew vivid as it cried for vengeance. Why should it change like that? I knew the sun had not come out; it could only be because the second door behind it had been opened and shut on the garden. But if he had gone out and seen his enemy then, he would have raised the alarm then; and it was some time afterwards that the fracas occurred. I began to feel he had gone out to do something ... to prepare something ... but as to when I was certain, that is a different matter. I knew that right at the end he was trying to hypnotize me, to master me by the black art of eyes like talismans and a voice like an incantation. That's what he used to do with old Aylmer, no doubt. But it wasn't only the way he said it, it was what he said. It was the religion and philosophy of it.'

'I'm afraid I'm a practical man,' said the doctor with gruff humour, 'and I don't bother much about religion and philosophy.'

'You'll never be a practical man till you do,' said Father Brown. 'Look here, doctor; you know me pretty well; I think you know I'm not a bigot. You know I know there are all sorts in all religions; good men in bad ones and bad men in good ones. But there's just one little fact I've learned simply as a practical man, an entirely practical point, that I've picked up by experience, like the tricks of an animal or the trade-mark of a good wine. I've scarcely ever met a criminal who philosophized at all, who didn't philosophize along those lines of orientalism and recurrence and reincarnation, and the wheel of destiny and the serpent biting its own tail. I have found merely in practice that there is a curse on the servants of that serpent; on their belly shall they go and the dust shall they eat; and there was never a blackguard or a profligate born who could not talk that sort of spirituality. It may not be like that in its real religious origins; but here in our working world it is the religion of rascals; and I knew it was a rascal who was speaking.'

'Why,' said Boyne, 'I should have thought that a rascal could pretty well profess any religion he chose.'

'Yes,' assented the other; 'he could profess any religion; that is he could pretend to any religion, if it was all a pretence. If it was mere mechanical hypocrisy and nothing else, no doubt it could be done by a mere mechanical hypocrite. Any sort of mask can be put on any sort of face. Anybody can learn certain phrases or state verbally that he holds certain views. I can go out into the street and state that I am a Wesleyan Methodist or a Sandemanian, though I fear in no very convincing accent. But we are talking about an artist; and for the enjoyment of the artist the mask must be to some extent moulded on the face. What he makes outside him must correspond to something inside him; he can only make his effects out of some of the materials of his soul. I suppose he could have said he was a Wesleyan Methodist; but he could never be an eloquent Methodist as he can be an eloquent mystic and fatalist. I am talking of the sort of ideal such a man thinks of if he really tries to be idealistic. It was his whole game with me to be as idealistic as possible; and whenever that is attempted by that sort of man, you will generally find it is that sort of ideal. That sort of man may be dripping with gore; but he will always be able to tell you quite sincerely that Buddhism is better than Christianity. Nay, he will tell you quite sincerely that Buddhism is more Christian than Christianity. That alone is enough to throw a hideous and ghastly ray of light on his notion of Christianity.'

'Upon my soul,' said the doctor, laughing, 'I can't make out whether you're denouncing or defending him.'

'It isn't defending a man to say he is a genius,' said Father Brown. 'Far from it. And it is simply a psychological fact that an artist will betray himself by some sort of sincerity. Leonardo da Vinci cannot draw as if he couldn't draw. Even if he tried, it will always be a strong parody of a weak thing. This man would have made something much too fearful and wonderful out of the Wesleyan Methodist.'

When the priest went forth again and set his face homeward, the cold had grown more intense and yet was somehow intoxicating. The trees stood up like silver candelabra of some incredible cold candlemas of purification. It was a piercing cold, like that silver sword of pure pain that once pierced the very heart of purity. But it was not a killing cold, save in the sense of seeming to kill all the mortal obstructions to our immortal and immeasurable vitality. The pale green sky of twilight, with one star

like the star of Bethlehem, seemed by some strange contradiction to be a cavern of clarity. It was as if there could
be a green furnace of cold which wakened all things to life
like warmth, and that the deeper they went into those cold
crystalline colours the more were they light like winged
creatures and clear like coloured glass. It tingled with
truth and it divided truth from error with a blade like ice;
but all that was left had never felt so much alive. It was as
if all joy were a jewel in the heart of an iceberg. The priest
hardly understood his own mood as he advanced deeper
and deeper into the green gloaming, drinking deeper and
deeper draughts of that virginal vivacity of the air. Some
forgotten muddle and morbidity seemed to be left behind,
or wiped out as the snow had painted out the footprints of
the man of blood. As he shuffled homewards through the
snow, he muttered to himself: 'And yet he is right enough
about there being a white magic, if he only knows where
to look for it.'

Cambric Tea

Marjorie Bowen

The situation was bizarre; the accurately trained mind of
Bevis Holroyd was impressed foremost by this; that the
opening of a door would turn it into tragedy.

'I am afraid I can't stay,' he had said pleasantly, hu-
mouring a sick man; he was too young and had not been
long enough completely successful to have a professional
manner but a certain balanced tolerance just showed in his
attitude to this prostrate creature.

'I've got a good many claims on my time,' he added,
'and I'm afraid it would be impossible. And it isn't the
least necessary, you know. You're quite all right. I'll come
back after Christmas if you really think it worth while.'

The patient opened one eye; he was lying flat on his
back in a deep, wide-fashioned bed hung with a thick,

dark, silk-lined tapestry; the room was dark for there were thick curtains of the same material drawn half across the windows, rigidly excluding all save a moiety of the pallid winter light; to make his examination Dr Holroyd had had to snap on the electric light that stood on the bedside table; he thought it a dreary unhealthy room, but had hardly found it worthwhile to say as much.

The patient opened one eye; the other lid remained fluttering feebly over an immobile orb.

He said in a voice both hoarse and feeble:

'But, doctor, I'm being poisoned.'

Professional curiosity and interest masked by genial incredulity instantly quickened the doctor's attention.

'My dear sir,' he smiled, 'poisoned by this nasty bout of 'flu you mean, I suppose – '

'No,' said the patient, faintly and wearily dropping both lids over his blank eyes, 'by my wife.'

'That's an ugly sort of fancy for you to get hold of,' replied the doctor instantly. 'Acute depression – we must see what we can do for you – '

The sick man opened both eyes now; he even slightly raised his head as he replied, not without dignity:

'I fetched you from London, Dr Holroyd, that you might deal with my case impartially – from the local man there is no hope of that, he is entirely impressed by my wife.'

Dr Holroyd made a movement as if to protest but a trembling sign from the patient made him quickly subsist.

'Please let me speak. *She* will come in soon and I shall have no chance. I sent for you secretly, she knows nothing about that. I had heard you very well spoken of – as an authority on this sort of thing. You made a name over the Pluntre murder case as witness for the Crown.'

'I don't specialize in murder,' said Dr Holroyd, but his keen handsome face was alight with interest. 'And I don't care much for this kind of case – Sir Harry.'

'But you've taken it on,' murmured the sick man. 'You couldn't abandon me now.'

'I'll get you into a nursing home,' said the doctor cheerfully, 'and there you'll dispel all these ideas.'

'And when the nursing home has cured me I'm to come back to my wife for her to begin again?'

Dr Holroyd bent suddenly and sharply over the sombre bed. With his right hand he deftly turned on the electric lamp and tipped back the coral silk shade so that the bleached acid light fell full over the patient lying on his back on the big fat pillows.

'Look here,' said the doctor, 'what you say is pretty serious.'

And the two men stared at each other, the patient examining his physician as acutely as his physician examined him.

Bevis Holroyd was still a young man with a look of peculiar energy and austere intelligence that heightened by contrast purely physical dark good looks that many men would have found sufficient passport to success; resolution, dignity, and a certain masculine sweetness, serene and strong, different from feminine sweetness, marked his demeanour which was further softened by a quick humour and a sensitive judgment.

The patient, on the other hand, was a man of well past middle age, light, flabby and obese with a flaccid, fallen look about his large face which was blurred and dimmed by the colours of ill health, being one pasty livid hue that threw into unpleasant relief the grey speckled red of his scant hair.

Altogether an unpleasing man, but of a certain fame and importance that had induced the rising young doctor to come at once when hastily summoned to Strangeways Manor House; a man of a fine, renowned family, a man of repute as a scholar, an essayist who had once been a politician who was rather above politics; a man whom Dr Holroyd only knew vaguely by reputation, but who seemed to him symbolical of all that was staid, respectable, and stolid.

And this man blinked up at him and whimpered:

'My wife is poisoning me.'

Dr Holroyd sat back and snapped off the electric light.

'What makes you think so?' he asked sharply.

'To tell you that,' came the laboured voice of the sick man, 'I should have to tell you my story.'

'Well, if you want me to take this up –'

'I sent for you to do that, doctor.'

'Well, how do you think you are being poisoned?'

'Arsenic, of course.'

'Oh? And how administered?'

Again the patient looked up with one eye, seeming too fatigued to open the other.

'Cambric tea,' he replied.

And Dr Holroyd echoed:

'Cambric tea!' with a soft amazement and interest.

Cambric tea had been used as the medium for arsenic in the Pluntre case and the expression had become famous; it was Bevis Holroyd who had discovered the doses in the cambric tea and who had put his finger on this pale beverage as the means of murder.

'Very possibly,' continued Sir Harry, 'the Pluntre case made her think of it.'

'For God's sake, don't,' said Dr Holroyd; for in that hideous affair the murderer had been a woman; and to see a woman on trial for her life, to see a woman sentenced to death, was not an experience he wished to repeat.

'Lady Strangeways,' continued the sick man, 'is much younger than I – I over persuaded her to marry me, she was at that time very much attracted by a man of

151

her own age, but he was in a poor position and she was ambitious.'

He paused, wiped his quivering lips on a silk handkerchief, and added faintly:

'Lately our marriage has been extremely unhappy. The man she preferred is now prosperous, successful, and unmarried – she wishes to dispose of me that she may marry her first choice.'

'Have you proof of any of this?'

'Yes. I know she buys arsenic. I know she reads books on poisons. I know she is eating her heart out for this other man.'

'Forgive me, Sir Harry,' replied the doctor, 'but have you no near friend nor relation to whom you can confide your – suspicions?'

'No one,' said the sick man impatiently. 'I have lately come from the East and am out of touch with people. Besides I want a doctor, a doctor with skill in this sort of thing. I thought from the first of the Pluntre case and of you.'

Bevis Holroyd sat back quietly; it was then that he thought of the situation as bizarre; the queerness of the whole thing was vividly before him, like a twisted figure on a gem – a carving at once writhing and immobile.

'Perhaps,' continued Sir Harry wearily, 'you are married, doctor?'

'No.' Dr Holroyd slightly smiled; his story was something like the sick man's story but taken from another angle; when he was very poor and unknown he had loved a girl who had preferred a wealthy man; she had gone out to India, ten years ago, and he had never seen her since; he remembered this, with sharp distinctness, and in the same breath he remembered that he still loved this girl; it was, after all, a common-place story.

Then his mind swung to the severe professional aspect of the case; he had thought that his patient, an unhealthy type of man, was struggling with a bad attack of influenza and the resultant depression and weakness, but then he had never thought, of course, of poison, nor looked nor tested for poison.

The man might be lunatic, he might be deceived, he might be speaking the truth; the fact that he was a mean, unpleasant beast ought not to weigh in the matter; Dr Holroyd had some enjoyable Christmas holidays in prospect and now he was beginning to feel that he ought to give these up to stay and investigate this case; for he could readily see that it was one in which the local doctor would be quite useless.

'You must have a nurse,' he said, rising.

But the sick man shook his head.

'I don't wish to expose my wife more than need be,' he grumbled. 'Can't you manage the affair yourself?'

As this was the first hint of decent feeling he had shown, Bevis Holroyd forgave him his brusque rudeness.

'Well, I'll stay the night anyhow,' he conceded.

And then the situation changed, with the opening of a door, from the bizarre to the tragic.

This door opened in the far end of the room and admitted a bloom of bluish winter light from some uncurtained, high-windowed corridor; the chill impression was as if invisible snow had entered the shaded, dun, close apartment.

And against this background appeared a woman in a smoke-coloured dress with some long lace about the shoulders and a high comb; she held a little tray carrying jugs and a glass of crystal in which the cold light splintered.

Dr Holroyd stood in his usual attitude of attentive courtesy, and then, as the patient, feebly twisting his gross head from the fat pillow, said:

'My wife – doctor –' he recognized in Lady Strangeways the girl to whom he had once been engaged in marriage, the woman he still loved.

'This is Doctor Holroyd,' added Sir Harry. 'Is that cambric tea you have there?'

She inclined her head to the stranger by her husband's bed as if she had never seen him before, and he, taking his cue, and for many other reasons, was silent.

'Yes, this is your cambric tea,' she said to her husband. 'You like it just now, don't you? How do you find Sir Harry, Dr Holroyd?'

There were two jugs on the tray; one of crystal half full of cold milk, and one of white porcelain full of hot water; Lady Strangeways proceeded to mix these fluids in equal proportions and gave the resultant drink to her husband, helping him first to sit up in bed.

'I think that Sir Harry has a nasty turn of influenza,' answered the doctor mechanically. 'He wants me to stay. I've promised till the morning, anyhow.'

'That will be a pleasure and a relief,' said Lady Strangeways gravely. 'My husband has been ill some time and seems so much worse than he need – for influenza.'

The patient, feebly sipping his cambric tea, grinned queerly at the doctor.

'So much worse – you see, doctor!' he muttered.

'It is good of you to stay,' continued Lady Strangeways equally. 'I will see about your room, you must be as comfortable as possible.'

She left as she had come, a shadow-coloured figure retreating to a chill light.

The sick man held up his glass as if he gave a toast.

'You see! Cambric tea!'

And Bevis Holroyd was thinking: does she not want to know me? Does he know what we once were to each other? How comes she to be married to this man – her husband's name was Custiss – and the horror of the situation shook the calm that was his both from character and training; he went to the window and looked out on the bleached park; light, slow snow was falling, a dreary dance over the frozen grass and before the grey corpses that paled, one behind the other, to the distance shrouded in colourless mist.

The thin voice of Harry Strangeways recalled him to the bed.

'Would you like to take a look at this, doctor?' He held out the half drunk glass of milk and water.

'I've no means of making a test here,' said Dr Holroyd, troubled. 'I brought a few things, nothing like that.'

'You are not so far from Harley Street,' said Sir Harry. 'My car can fetch everything you want by this afternoon – or perhaps you would like to go yourself?'

'Yes,' replied Bevis Holroyd sternly. 'I would rather go myself.'

His trained mind had been rapidly covering the main aspects of his problem and he had instantly seen that it was better for Lady Strangeways to have this case in his hands. He was sure there was some hideous, fantastic hallucination on the part of Sir Harry, but it was better for Lady Strangeways to leave the matter in the hands of one who was friendly towards her. He rapidly found and

washed a medicine bottle from among the sick room para-
phernalia and poured it full of the cambric tea, casting
away the remainder.

'Why did you drink any?' he asked sharply.

'I don't want her to think that I guess,' whispered Sir
Harry. 'Do you know, doctor, I have a lot of her love
letters – written by – '

Dr Holroyd cut him short.

'I couldn't listen to this sort of thing behind Lady
Strangeways's back,' he said quickly. 'That is between
you and her. My job is to get you well. I'll try and do that.'

And he considered, with a faint disgust, how repulsive
this man looked sitting up with pendant jowl and drooping cheeks and discoloured, pouchy eyes sunk in pads of
unhealthy flesh and above the spiky crown of Judas-col-
oured hair.

Perhaps a woman, chained to this man, living with him,
blocked and thwarted by him, might be wrought upon to –

Dr Holroyd shuddered inwardly and refused to continue his reflection.

As he was leaving the gaunt sombre house about which
there was something definitely blank and unfriendly, a shrine
in which the sacred flames had flickered out so long ago that
the lamps were blank and cold, he met Lady Strangeways.

She was in the wide entrance hall standing by the wood
fire that but faintly dispersed the gloom of the winter

morning and left untouched the shadows in the rafters of the open roof.

Now he would not, whether she wished or no, deny her; he stopped before her, blocking out her poor remnant of light.

'Mollie,' he said gently, 'I don't quite understand – you married a man named Custiss in India.'

'Yes. Harry had to take this name when he inherited this place. We've been home three years from the East, but lived so quietly here that I don't suppose anyone has heard of us.'

She stood between him and the firelight, a shadow among the shadows; she was much changed; in her thinness and pallor, in her restless eyes and nervous mouth he could read signs of discontent, even of unhappiness.

'I never heard of you,' said Dr Holroyd truthfully. 'I didn't want to. I liked to keep my dreams.'

Her hair was yet the lovely cedar wood hue, silver, soft, and gracious; her figure had those fluid lines of grace that he believed he had never seen equalled.

'Tell me,' she added abruptly, 'what is the matter with my husband? He has been ailing like this for a year or so.'

With a horrid lurch of his heart that was usually so steady, Dr Holroyd remembered the bottle of milk and water in his pocket.

'Why do you give him that cambric tea?' he counter questioned.

'He will have it – he insists that I make it for him – '

'Mollie,' said Dr Holroyd quickly, 'you decided against me, ten years ago, but that is no reason why we should not be friends now – tell me, frankly, are you happy with this man?'

'You have seen him,' she replied slowly. 'He seemed different ten years ago. I honestly was attracted by his scholarship and his learning as well as – other things.'

Bevis Holroyd needed to ask no more; she was wretched, imprisoned in a mistake as a fly in amber; and those love letters? Was there another man?

As he stood silent, with a dark reflective look on her weary brooding face, she spoke again:

'You are staying?'

'Oh yes,' he said, he was staying, there was nothing else for him to do.

'It is Christmas week,' she reminded him wistfully. 'It will be very dull, perhaps painful, for you.'

'I think I ought to stay.'

Sir Harry's car was announced; Bevis Holroyd, gliding over frozen roads to London, was absorbed with this sudden problem that, like a mountain out of a plain, had suddenly risen to confront him out of his level life.

The sight of Mollie (he could not think of her by that sick man's name) had roused in him tender memories and poignant emotions and the position in which he found her and his own juxtaposition to her and her husband had the same devastating effect on him as a mine sprung beneath the feet of an unwary traveller.

London was deep in the whirl of a snow storm and the light that penetrated over the grey roof tops to the ugly slip of a laboratory at the back of his consulting rooms was chill and forbidding.

Bevis Holroyd put the bottle of milk on a marble slab and sat back in the easy chair watching that dreary chase of snow flakes across the dingy London pane.

He was thinking of past springs, of violets long dead, of roses long since dust, of hours that had slipped away like lengths of golden silk rolled up, of the long ago when he had loved Mollie and Mollie had seemed to love him; then he thought of that man in the big bed who had said:

'My wife is poisoning me.'

Late that afternoon Dr Holroyd, with his suit case and a professional bag, returned to Strangeways Manor House in Sir Harry's car; the bottle of cambric tea had gone to a friend, a noted analyst; somehow Doctor Holroyd had not felt able to do this task himself; he was very fortunate, he felt, in securing this old solitary and his promise to do the work before Christmas.

As he arrived at Strangeways Manor House which stood isolated and well away from a public high road where a lonely spur of the weald of Kent drove into the Sussex marshes, it was in a blizzard of snow that effaced the landscape and gave the murky outlines of the house an air of unreality, and Bevis Holroyd experienced that sensation he had so often heard of and read about, but which so far his cool mind had dismissed as a fiction.

He did really feel as if he was in an evil dream; as the snow changed the values of the scene, altering distances and shapes, so this meeting with Mollie, under these circumstances, had suddenly changed the life of Bevis Holroyd.

He had so resolutely and so definitely put this woman out of his life and mind, deliberately refusing to make enquiries about her, letting all knowledge of her cease with the letter in which she had written from India and announced her marriage.

And now, after ten years, she had crossed his path in this ghastly manner, as a woman her husband accused of attempted murder.

The sick man's words of a former lover disturbed him profoundly; was it himself who was referred to? Yet the love letters must be from another man for he had not corresponded with Mollie since her marriage, not for ten years.

He had never felt any bitterness towards Mollie for her desertion of a poor, struggling doctor, and he had always believed in the integral nobility of her character under the timidity of conventionality; but the fact remained that she had played him false – what if that *had* been 'the little rift within the lute' that had now indeed silenced the music!

With a sense of bitter depression he entered the gloomy old house; how different was this from the pleasant ordinary Christmas he had been rather looking forward to, the jolly homely atmosphere of good fare, dancing, and friends!

When he had telephoned to these friends excusing himself his regret had been genuine and the cordial 'bad luck!' had had a poignant echo in his own heart; bad luck indeed, bad luck –

She was waiting for him in the hall that a pale young man was decorating with boughs of prickly stiff holly that stuck stiffly behind the dark heavy pictures.

He was introduced as the secretary and said gloomily:

'Sir Harry wished everything to go on as usual, though I am afraid he is very ill indeed.'

Yes, the patient had been seized by another violent attack of illness during Dr Holroyd's absence; the young man went at once upstairs and found Sir Harry in a deep sleep and a rather nervous local doctor in attendance.

An exhaustive discussion of the case with this doctor threw no light on anything, and Dr Holroyd, leaving in charge an extremely sensible-looking housekeeper who was Sir Harry's preferred nurse, returned, worried and irritated, to the hall where Lady Strangeways now sat alone before the big fire.

She offered him a belated but fresh cup of tea.

'Why did you come?' she asked as if she roused herself from deep reverie.

'Why? Because your husband sent for me.'

'He says you offered to come; he has told everyone in the house that.'

'But I never heard of the man before today.'

'You had heard of me. He seems to think that you came here to help me.'

'He cannot be saying that,' returned Dr Holroyd sternly, and he wondered desperately if Mollie was lying, if she had invented this to drive him out of the house.

'Do you want me here?' he demanded.

'I don't know,' she replied dully and confirmed his suspicions; probably there was another man and she wished him out of the way; but he could not go, out of pity towards her he could not go.

'Does he know we once knew each other?' he asked.

'No,' she replied faintly, 'therefore it seems such a curious chance that he should have sent for you, of all men!'

'It would have been more curious,' he responded grimly, 'if I had heard that you were here with a sick husband and had thrust myself in to doctor him! Strangeways must be crazy to spread such a tale and if he doesn't know we are old friends it becomes nonsense!'

'I often think that Harry is crazy,' said Lady Strange-ways wearily; she took a rose silk-lined work basket, full of pretty trifles, on her knee, and began winding a skein of rose-coloured silk; she looked so frail, so sad, so life-less that the heart of Bevis Holroyd was torn with bitter pity.

'Now I am here I want to help you,' he said earnestly. 'I am staying for that, to help you – '

She looked up at him with a wistful appeal in her fair face.

'I'm worried,' she said simply. 'I've lost some letters I valued very much – I think they have been stolen.'

Dr Holroyd drew back; the love letters; the letters the husband had found, that were causing all his ugly suspicions.

'My poor Mollie!' he exclaimed impulsively. 'What sort of a coil have you got yourself into!'

As if this note of pity was unendurable, she rose impul-sively, scattering the contents of her work basket, drop-ping the skein of silk, and hastened away down the dark hall.

Bevis Holroyd stooped mechanically to pick up the hurled objects and saw among them a small white packet, folded, but opened at one end; this packet seemed to have fallen out of a needle case of gold silk.

Bevis Holroyd had pounced on it and thrust it in his

pocket just as the pale secretary returned with his thin arms most incongruously full of mistletoe.

'This will be a dreary Christmas for you, Dr Holroyd,' he said with the air of one who forces himself to make conversation. 'No doubt you had some pleasant plans in view – we are all so pleased that Lady Strangeways had a friend to come and look after Sir Harry during the holidays.'

'Who told you I was a friend?' asked Dr Holroyd brusquely. 'I certainly knew Lady Strangeways before she was married –'

The pale young man cut in crisply:

'Oh, Lady Strangeways told me so herself.'

Bevis Holroyd was bewildered; why did she tell the secretary what she did not tell her husband? – both the indiscretion and the reserve seemed equally foolish.

Languidly hanging up his sprays and bunches of mistletoe the pallid young man, whose name was Garth Deane, continued his aimless remarks.

'This is really not a very cheerful house, Dr Holroyd – I'm interested in Sir Harry's oriental work or I should not remain. Such a very unhappy marriage! I often think,' he added regardless of Bevis Holroyd's darkling glance, 'that it would be very unpleasant indeed for Lady Strangeways if anything happened to Sir Harry.'

'Whatever do you mean, sir?' asked the doctor angrily.

The secretary was not at all discomposed.

'Well, one lives in the house, one has nothing much to do – and one notices.'

Perhaps, thought the young man in anguish, the sick husband had been talking to this creature, perhaps the creature *had* really noticed something.

'I'll go up to my patient,' said Bevis Holroyd briefly, not daring to anger one who might be an important witness in this mystery that was at present so unfathomable.

Mr Deane gave a sickly grin over the lovely pale leaves and berries he was holding.

'I'm afraid he is very bad, doctor.'

As Bevis Holroyd left the room he passed Lady Strangeways; she looked blurred, like a pastel drawing that has been shaken; the fingers she kept locked on her bosom; she had flung a silver fur over her shoulders that accentuated her ethereal look of blonde, pearl, and amber hues.

'I've come back for my work basket,' she said. 'Will you go up to my husband? He is ill again – '

'Have you been giving him anything?' asked Dr Holroyd as quietly as he could.

'Only some cambric tea, he insisted on that.'

'Don't give him anything – leave him alone. He is in my charge now, do you understand?'

She gazed up at him with frightened eyes that had been newly washed by tears.

'Why are you so unkind to me?' she quivered.

She looked so ready to fall that he could not resist the temptation to put his hand protectingly on her arm, so that, as she stood in the low doorway leading to the stairs, he appeared to be supporting her drooping weight.

'Have I not said that I am here to help you, Mollie?'

The secretary slipped out from the shadows behind them, his arms still full of winter evergreens.

'There is too much foliage,' he smiled, and the smile told that he had seen and heard.

Bevis Holroyd went angrily upstairs; he felt as if an invisible net was being dragged closely round him, something which, from being a cobweb, would become a cable; this air of mystery, of horror in the big house, this sly secretary, these watchful-looking servants, the nervous village doctor ready to credit anything, the lovely agitated woman who was the woman he had long so romantically loved, and the sinister sick man with his diabolic accusations, a man Bevis Holroyd had, from the first moment, hated – all these people in these dark surroundings affected the young man with a miasma of apprehension, gloom, and dread.

After a few hours of it he was nearer to losing his nerve than he had ever been; that must be because of Mollie, poor darling Mollie caught into all this nightmare.

And outside the bells were ringing across the snow, practising for Christmas Day; the sound of them was to

Bevis Holroyd what the sounds of the real world are when breaking into a sleeper's thick dreams.

The patient sat up in bed, fondling the glass of odious cambric tea.

'Why do you take the stuff?' demanded the doctor angrily.

'She won't let me off, she thrusts it on me,' whispered Sir Harry.

Bevis Holroyd noticed, not for the first time since he had come into the fell atmosphere of this dark house that enclosed the piteous figure of the woman he loved, that husband and wife were telling different tales; on one side lay a burden of careful lying.

'Did she –' continued the sick man, 'speak to you of her lost letters?'

The young doctor looked at him sternly.

'Why should Lady Strangeways make a confidante of me?' he asked. 'Do you know that she was a friend of mine ten years ago before she married you?'

'Was she? How curious! But you met like strangers.'

'The light in this room is very dim – '

'Well, never mind about that, whether you knew her or not –' Sir Harry gasped out in a sudden snarl. 'The woman is a murderess, and you'll have to bear witness to it – I've got her letters, here under my pillow, and Garth Deane is watching her – '

'Ah, a spy! I'll have no part in this, Sir Harry. You'll call another doctor – '

'No, it's your case, you'll make the best of it – My God, I'm dying, I think – '

He fell back in such a convulsion of pain that Bevis Holroyd forgot everything in administering to him. The rest of that day and all that night the young doctor was shut up with his patient, assisted by the secretary and the housekeeper.

And when, in the pallid light of Christmas Eve morning, he went downstairs to find Lady Strangeways, he knew that the sick man was suffering from arsenic poison, that the packet taken from Mollie's work box was arsenic, and it was only an added horror when he was called to the telephone to learn that a stiff dose of the poison had been found in the specimen of cambric tea.

He believed that he could save the husband and thereby the wife also, but he did not think he could close the sick man's mouth; the deadly hatred of Sir Harry was leading up to an accusation of attempted murder; of that he was sure, and there was the man Deane to back him up.

He sent for Mollie, who had not been near her husband all night, and when she came, pale, distracted, huddled in her white fur, he said grimly:

'Look here, Mollie, I promised that I'd help you and I mean to, though it isn't going to be as easy as I thought, but you have got to be frank with me.'

'But I have nothing to conceal – '

'The name of the other man – '

'The other man?'

'The man who wrote those letters your husband has under his pillow.'

'Oh, Harry has them!' she cried in pain. 'That man Deane stole them then! Bevis, they are your letters of the olden days that I have always cherished.'

'*My* letters!'

'Yes, do you think that there has ever been anyone else?'

'But he says – Mollie, there is a trap or trick here, someone is lying furiously. Your husband is being poisoned.'

'Poisoned?'

'By arsenic given in that cambric tea. And he knows it. And he accuses you.'

She stared at him in blank incredulity, then she slipped forward in her chair and clutched the big arm.

'Oh, God,' she muttered in panic terror. 'He always swore that he'd be revenged on me – because he knew that I never cared for him – '

But Bevis Holroyd recoiled; he did not dare listen, he did not dare believe.

'I've warned you,' he said, 'for the sake of the old days, Mollie – '

A light step behind them and they were aware of the secretary creeping out of the embrowning shadows.

'A cold Christmas,' he said, rubbing his hands together. 'A really cold, seasonable Christmas. We are almost snowed in – and Sir Harry would like to see you, Dr Holroyd.'

'I have only just left him – '

Bevis Holroyd looked at the despairing figure of the woman, crouching in her chair; he was distracted, over-wrought, near to losing his nerve.

'He wants particularly to see you,' cringed the secretary.

Mollie looked back at Bevis Holroyd, her lips moved twice in vain before she could say: 'Go to him.'

The doctor went slowly upstairs and the secretary followed. Sir Harry was now flat on his back, staring at the dark tapestry curtains of his bed.

'I'm dying,' he announced as the doctor bent over him.

'Nonsense. I am not going to allow you to die.'

'You won't be able to help yourself. I've brought you here to see me die.'

'What do you mean?'

'I've a surprise for you too, a Christmas present. These letters now, these love letters of my wife's – what name do you think is on them?'

'Your mind is giving way, Sir Harry.'

'Not at all – come nearer, Deane – the name is Bevis Holroyd.'

'Then they are letters ten years old. Letters written before your wife met you.'

The sick man grinned with infinite malice.

'Maybe. But there are no dates on them and the envelopes are all destroyed. And I, as a dying man, shall swear to their recent date – I, as a foully murdered man.'

'You are wandering in your mind,' said Bevis Holroyd quietly. 'I refuse to listen to you any further.'

'You shall listen to me. I brought you here to listen to me. I've got you. Here's my will, Deane's got that, in which I denounced you both, there are your letters, every one thinks that *she* put you in charge of the case, every one knows that you know all about arsenic in cambric tea through the Pluntre case, and every one will know that I died of arsenic poisoning.'

The doctor allowed him to talk himself out; indeed it would have been difficult to check the ferocity of his malicious energy.

The plot was ingenious, the invention of a slightly insane, jealous recluse who hated his wife and hated the man she had never ceased to love; Bevis Holroyd could see the nets very skillfully drawn round him; but the main issue of the mystery remained untouched; who *was* administering the arsenic?

The young man glanced across the sombre bed to the dark figure of the secretary.

'What is your place in all this farrago, Mr Deane?' he asked sternly.

'I'm Sir Harry's friend,' answered the other stubbornly, 'and I'll bring witness any time against Lady Strangeways. I've tried to circumvent her – '

'Stop,' cried the doctor. 'You think that Lady Strangeways is poisoning her husband and that I am her accomplice?'

The sick man, who had been looking with bitter malice from one to another, whispered hoarsely:

'That is what you think, isn't it, Deane?'

'I'll say what I think at the proper time,' said the secretary obstinately.

'No doubt you are being well paid for your share in this.'

'I've remembered his services in my will,' smiled Sir Harry grimly. 'You can adjust your differences then, Dr Holroyd, when I'm dead, *poisoned*, *murdered*. It will be a pretty story, a nice scandal, you and she in the house together, the letters, the cambric tea!'

An expression of ferocity dominated him, then he made an effort to dominate this and to speak in his usual suave stilted manner:

'You must admit that we shall all have a very Happy Christmas, doctor.'

Bevis Holroyd was looking at the secretary, who stood at the other side of the bed, cringing, yet somehow in the attitude of a man ready to pounce; Dr Holroyd wondered if this was the murderer.

'Why,' he asked quietly to gain time, 'did you hatch this plan to ruin a man you had never seen before?'

'I always hated you,' replied the sick man faintly. 'Mollie never forgot you, you see, and she never allowed *me* to forget that she never forgot you. And then I found those letters she had cherished.'

'You are a very wicked man,' said the doctor dryly, 'but it will all come to nothing, for I am not going to allow you to die.'

'You won't be able to help yourself,' replied the patient. 'I'm dying, I tell you. I shall die on Christmas Day.'

He turned his head towards the secretary and added:

'Send my wife up to me.'

'No,' interrupted Dr Holroyd strongly. 'She shall not come near you again.'

Sir Harry Strangeways ignored this.

'Send her up,' he repeated.

'I will bring her, sir.'

The secretary left, with a movement suggestive of flight, and Bevis Holroyd stood rigid, waiting, thinking, looking at the ugly man who now had closed his eyes and lay as if insensible. He was certainly very ill, dying perhaps, and he certainly had been poisoned by arsenic given in cambric tea, and, as certainly, a terrible scandal and a terrible danger would threaten with his death; the letters were *not* dated, the marriage was notoriously

174

unhappy, and he, Bevis Holroyd, was associated in every one's mind with a murder case in which this form of poison, given in this manner, had been used.

Drops of moisture stood out on the doctor's forehead; sure that if he could clear himself it would be very difficult for Mollie to do so; how could even he himself in his soul swear to her innocence!

Of course he must get the woman out of the house at once, he must have another doctor from town, nurses – but could this be done in time; if the patient died on his hands would he not be only bringing witnesses to his own discomfiture? And the right people, his own friends, were difficult to get hold of now, at Christmas time.

He longed to go in search of Mollie – she must at least be got away, but how, without a scandal, without a suspicion?

He longed to have the matter out with this odious secretary, but he dared not leave his patient.

Lady Strangeways returned with Garth Deane and seated herself, mute, shadowy, with eyes full of panic, on the other side of the sombre bed.

'Is he going to live?' she presently whispered as she watched Bevis Holroyd ministering to her unconscious husband.

'We must see that he does,' he answered grimly.

All through that Christmas Eve and the bitter night to the stark dawn when the church bells broke ghastly on their wan senses did they tend the sick man who only came to his senses to grin at them in malice.

Once Bevis Holroyd asked the pallid woman:

'What was that white packet you had in your work box?'

And she replied:

'I never had such a packet.'

And he:

'I must believe you.'

But he did not send for the other doctors and nurses, he did not dare.

The Christmas bells seemed to rouse the sick man from his deadly swoon.

'You can't save me,' he said with indescribable malice. 'I shall die and put you both in the dock –'

Mollie Strangeways sank down beside the bed and began to cry, and Garth Deane, who by his master's express desire had been in and out of the room all night, stopped and looked at her with a peculiar expression. Sir Harry looked at her also.

'Don't cry,' he gasped, 'this is Christmas Day. We ought all to be happy – bring me my cambric tea – do you hear?'

She rose mechanically and left the room to take in the tray with the fresh milk and water that the housekeeper had placed softly on the table outside the door; for all through the nightmare vigil, the sick man's cry had been for 'cambric tea'. As he sat up in bed feebly sipping the vapid and odious drink the tortured woman's nerves slipped her control.

'I can't endure those bells, I wish they would stop those bells!' she cried and ran out of the room.

Bevis Holroyd instantly followed her; and now as suddenly as it had sprung on him, the fell little drama disappeared, fled like a poison cloud out of the compass of his life.

Mollie was leaning against the closed window, her sick head resting against the mullions; through the casement showed, surprisingly, sunlight on the pure snow and blue sky behind the withered trees.

'Listen, Mollie,' said the young man resolutely. 'I'm sure he'll live if you are careful – you mustn't lose heart – '

The sick room door opened and the secretary slipped out.

He nervously approached the two in the window place.

'I can't stand this any longer,' he said through dry lips. 'I didn't know he meant to go so far, he is doing it himself, you know; he's got the stuff hidden in his bed, he puts it into the cambric tea, he's willing to die to spite you two, but I can't stand it any longer.'

'You've been abetting this!' cried the doctor.

MARJORIE BOWEN

'Not abetting,' smiled the secretary wanly. 'Just standing by. I found out by chance – and then he forced me to be silent – I had his will, you know, and I've destroyed it.'

With this the strange creature glided downstairs.

The doctor sprang at once to Sir Harry's room; the sick man was sitting up in the sombre bed and with a last effort was scattering a grain of powder into the glass of cambric tea.

With a look of baffled horror he saw Bevis Holroyd but the drink had already slipped down his throat; he fell back and hid his face, baulked at the last of his diabolic revenge.

When Bevis Holroyd left the dead man's chamber he found Mollie still leaning in the window; she was free, the sun was shining, it was Christmas Day.

As Dark as Christmas Gets

Lawrence Block

It was 9:54 in the morning when I got to the little bookshop on West 56th Street. Before I went to work for Leo Haig I probably wouldn't have bothered to look at my watch, if I was even wearing one in the first place, and the best I'd have been able to say was it was around ten o'clock. But Haig wanted me to be his legs and eyes, and sometimes his ears, nose and throat, and if he was going to play in Nero Wolfe's league, that meant I had to turn into Archie Goodwin, for Pete's sake, noticing everything and getting the details right and reporting conversations verbatim.

Well, forget that last part. My memory's getting better – Haig's right about that part – but what follows won't be word for word, because all I am is a human being. If you want a tape recorder, buy one.

There was a lot of fake snow in the window, and a Santa Claus doll in handcuffs, and some toy guns and knives, and a lot of mysteries with a Christmas theme, including the one by Fredric Brown where the murderer dresses up as a department store Santa. (Someone pulled that a year ago, put on a red suit and a white beard and shot a man at the corner of Broadway and 37th, and I told Haig how ingenious I thought it was. He gave me a look, left the room, and came back with a book. I read it – that's what I do when Haig hands me a book – and found out Brown had had the idea fifty years earlier. Which doesn't mean that's where the killer got the idea. The book's long out of print – the one I read was a paperback, and falling apart, not like the handsome hardcover copy in the window. And how many killers get their ideas out of old books?)

Now if you're a detective yourself you'll have figured out two things by now – the bookshop specialized in mysteries, and it was the Christmas season. And if you'd noticed the sign in the window you'd have made one more deduction, i.e., that they were closed.

I went down the half flight of steps and poked the buzzer. When nothing happened I poked it again, and eventually the door was opened by a little man with white hair and a white beard – all he needed was padding and a red suit, and someone to teach him to be jolly. 'I'm terribly

180

sorry,' he said, 'but I'm afraid we're closed. It's Christmas morning, and it's not even ten o'clock.'

'You called us,' I said, 'and it wasn't even nine o'clock.'

He took a good look at me, and light dawned. 'You're Harrison,' he said. 'And I know your first name, but I can't—'

'Chip,' I supplied.

'Of course. But where's Haig? I know he thinks he's Nero Wolfe, but he's not gone housebound, has he? He's been here often enough in the past.'

'Haig gets out and about,' I agreed, 'but Wolfe went all the way to Montana once, as far as that goes. What Wolfe refused to do was leave the house on business, and Haig's with him on that one. Besides, he just spawned some un-spawnable cichlids from Lake Chad, and you'd think the aquarium was a television set and they were showing *Midnight Blue*.'

'Fish.' He sounded more reflective than contemptuous. 'Well, at least you're here. That's something.' He locked the door and led me up a spiral staircase to a room full of books, and full as well with the residue of a party. There were empty glasses here and there, hors d'oeuvres trays that held nothing but crumbs, and a cut-glass dish with a sole remaining cashew.

'Christmas,' he said, and shuddered. 'I had a houseful of people here last night. All of them eating, all of them drinking, and many of them actually singing.' He made a

181

face. 'I didn't sing,' he said, 'but I certainly ate and drank. And eventually they all went home and I went upstairs to bed. I must have, because that's where I was when I woke up two hours ago.'

'But you don't remember.'

'Well, no,' he said, 'but then what would there be to remember? The guests leave and you're alone with vague feelings of sadness.' His gaze turned inward. 'If she'd stayed,' he said, 'I'd have remembered.'

'She?'

'Never mind. I awoke this morning, alone in my own bed. I swallowed some aspirin and came downstairs. I went into the library.'

'You mean this room?'

'This is the salesroom. These books are for sale.'

'Well, I figured. I mean, this is a bookshop.'

'You've never seen the library?' He didn't wait for an answer but turned to open a door and lead me down a hallway to another room twice the size of the first. It was lined with floor-to-ceiling hardwood shelves, and the shelves were filled with double rows of hardcover books. It was hard to identify the books, though, because all but one section was wrapped in plastic sheeting.

'This is my collection,' he announced. 'These books are not for sale. I'll only part with one if I've replaced it with a finer copy. Your employer doesn't collect, does he?'

'Haig? He's got thousands of books.'

'Yes, and he's bought some of them from me. But he doesn't give a damn about first editions. He doesn't care what kind of shape a book is in, or even if it's got a dust jacket. He'd as soon have a Grosset reprint or a book-club edition or even a paperback.'

'He just wants to read them.'

'It takes all kinds, doesn't it?' He shook his head in wonder. 'Last night's party filled this room as well as the salesroom. I put up plastic to keep the books from getting handled and possibly damaged. Or – how shall I put this?'

Any way you want, I thought. You're the client.

'Some of these books are extremely valuable,' he said. 'And my guests were all extremely reputable people, but many of them are good customers, and that means they're collectors. Ardent, even rabid collectors.'

'And you didn't want them stealing the books.'

'You're very direct,' he said. 'I suppose that's a useful quality in your line of work. But no, I didn't want to tempt anyone, especially when alcoholic indulgence might make temptation particularly difficult to resist.'

'So you hung up plastic sheets.'

'And came downstairs this morning to remove the plastic, and pick up some dirty glasses and clear some of the debris. I puttered around. I took down the plastic from this one section, as you can see. I did a bit of tidying. And then I saw it.'

'Saw what?'

He pointed to a set of glassed-in shelves, on top of which stood a three-foot row of leather-bound volumes. 'There,' he said. 'What do you see?'

'Leather-bound books, but – '

'Boxes,' he corrected. 'Wrapped in leather and stamped in gold, and each one holding a manuscript. They're fashioned to look like finely-bound books, but they're original manuscripts.'

'Very nice,' I said. 'I suppose they must be very rare.'

'They're unique.'

'That too.'

He made a face. 'One of a kind. The author's original manuscript, with corrections in his own hand. Most are typed, but the Elmore Leonard is handwritten. The Westlake, of course, is typed on that famous Smith-Corona manual portable of his. The Paul Kavanagh is the author's first novel. He only wrote three, you know.'

I didn't, but Haig would.

'They're very nice,' I said politely. 'And I don't suppose they're for sale.'

'Of course not. They're in the library. They're part of the collection.'

'Right,' I said, and paused for him to continue. When

he didn't I said, 'Uh, I was thinking. Maybe you could tell me ...'

'Why I summoned you here.' He sighed. 'Look at the boxed manuscript between the Westlake and the Kavanagh.'

'Between them?'

'Yes.'

'The Kavanagh is *Such Men are Dangerous,*' I said, 'and the Westlake is *Drowned Hopes*. But there's nothing at all between them but a three-inch gap.'

'Exactly,' he said.

'As Dark as It Gets,' I said. 'By Cornell Woolrich.'

Haig frowned. 'I don't know the book,' he said. 'Not under that title, not with Woolrich's name on it, nor William Irish or George Hopley. Those were his pen names.'

'I know,' I said. 'You don't know the book because it was never published. The manuscript was found among Woolrich's effects after his death.'

'There was a posthumous book, Chip.'

'Into the Night,' I said. 'Another writer completed it, writing replacement scenes for some that had gone missing in the original. It wound up being publishable.'

'It wound up being published,' Haig said. 'That's not necessarily the same thing. But this manuscript, *As Dark—*'

'As It Gets. It wasn't publishable, according to our client. Woolrich evidently worked on it over the years, and what survived him incorporated unresolved portions of several drafts. There are characters who die early on and then reappear with no explanation. There's supposed to be some great writing and plenty of Woolrich's trademark paranoid suspense, but it doesn't add up to a book, or even something that could be edited into a book. But to a collector – '

'Collectors,' Haig said heavily.

'Yes, sir. I asked what the manuscript was worth. He said, "Well, I paid five thousand dollars for it." That's verbatim, but don't ask me if the thing's worth more or less than that, because I don't know if he was bragging that he was a big spender or a slick trader.'

'It doesn't matter,' Haig said. 'The money's the least of it. He added it to his collection and he wants it back.'

'And the person who stole it,' I said, 'is either a friend or a customer or both.'

'And so he called us and not the police. The manuscript was there when the party started?'

'Yes.'

'And gone this morning?'

'Yes.'

'And there were how many in attendance?'

'Forty or fifty,' I said, 'including the caterer and her staff.'

'If the party was catered,' he mused, 'why was the room a mess when you saw it? Wouldn't the catering staff have cleaned up at the party's end?'

'I asked him that question myself. The party lasted longer than the caterer had signed on for. She hung around herself for a while after her employees packed it in, but she stopped working and became a guest. Our client was hoping she would stay.'

'But you just said she did.'

'After everybody else went home. He lives upstairs from the bookshop, and he was hoping for a chance to show her his living quarters.'

Haig shrugged. He's not quite the misogynist his idol is, but he hasn't been at it as long. Give him time. He said, 'Chip, it's hopeless. Fifty suspects?'

'Six.'

'How so?'

'By two o'clock,' I said, 'just about everybody had called it a night. The ones remaining got a reward.'

'And what was that?'

'Some fifty-year-old Armagnac, served in Waterford pony glasses. We counted the glasses, and there were seven of them. Six guests and the host.'

'And the manuscript?'

'Was still there at the time, and still sheathed in plastic. See, he'd covered all the boxed manuscripts, same as the books on the shelves. But the cut-glass ship's decanter was serving as a sort of bookend to the manuscript section, and he took off the plastic to get at it. And while he was at it he took out one of the manuscripts and showed it off to his guests.'

'Not the Woolrich, I don't suppose.'

'No, it was a Peter Straub novel, elegantly handwritten in a leatherbound journal. Straub collects Chandler, and our client had traded a couple of Chandler firsts for the manuscript, and he was proud of himself.'

'I shouldn't wonder.'

'But the Woolrich was present and accounted for when he took off the plastic wrap, and it may have been there when he put the Straub back. He didn't notice.'

'And this morning it was gone.'

'Yes.'

'Six suspects,' he said. 'Name them.'

I took out my notebook. 'Jon and Jayne Corn-Wallace,' I said. 'He's a retired stockbroker, she's an actress in a daytime drama. That's a soap opera.'

'Piffle.'

'Yes, sir. They've been friends of our client for years, and customers for about as long. They were mystery fans, and he got them started on first editions.'

'Including Woolrich?'

'He's a favorite of Jayne's. I gather Jon can take him or leave him.'

'I wonder which he did last night. Do the Corn-Wallaces collect manuscripts?'

'Just books. First editions, though they're starting to get interested in fancy bindings and limited editions. The one with a special interest in manuscripts is Zoltan Mihalyi.'

'The violinist?'

Trust Haig to know that. I'd never heard of him myself. 'A big mystery fan,' I said. 'I guess reading passes the time on those long concert tours.'

'I don't suppose a man can spend all his free hours with other men's wives,' Haig said. 'And who's to say that all the stories are true? He collects manuscripts, does he?'

'He was begging for a chance to buy the Straub, but our friend wouldn't sell.'

'Which would make him a likely suspect. Who else?'

'Philip Perigord.'

'The writer?'

'Right, and I didn't even know he was still alive. He hasn't written anything in years.'

'Almost twenty years. *More Than Murder* was published in 1980.'

Trust him to know that, too. 'Anyway,' I said, 'he didn't die. He didn't even stop writing. He just quit writing books. He went to Hollywood and became a screenwriter.'

'That's the same as stopping writing,' Haig reflected.

'It's very nearly the same as being dead. Does he collect books?'

'No.'

'Manuscripts?'

'No.'

'Perhaps he wanted the manuscripts for scrap paper,' Haig said. 'He could turn the pages over and write on their backs. Who else was present?'

'Edward Everett Stokes.'

'The small-press publisher. Bought out his partner, Geoffrey Poges, to became sole owner of Stokes-Poges Press.'

'They do limited editions, according to our client. Leather bindings, small runs, special tip-in sheets.'

'All well and good,' he said, 'but what's useful about Stokes-Poges is that they issue a reasonably priced trade edition of each title as well, and publish works otherwise unavailable, including collections of short fiction from otherwise uncollected writers.'

'Do they publish Woolrich?'

'All his work has been published by mainstream publishers, and all his stories collected. Is Stokes a collector himself?'

'Our client didn't say.'

'No matter. How many is that? The Corn-Wallaces, Zoltan Mihalyi, Philip Perigord, E. E. Stokes. And the sixth is –'

'Harriet Quinlan.'

He looked puzzled, then nodded in recognition. 'The literary agent.'

'She represents Perigord,' I said, 'or at least she would, if he ever went back to novel-writing. She's placed books with Stokes-Poges. And she may have left the party with Zoltan Mihalyi.'

'I don't suppose her client list includes the Woolrich estate. Or that she's a rabid collector of books and manuscripts.'

'He didn't say.'

'No matter. You said six suspects, Chip. I count seven.'

I ticked them off. 'Jon Corn-Wallace. Jayne Corn-Wallace. Zoltan Mihalyi. Philip Perigord. Edward Everett Stokes. Harriet Quinlan. Isn't that six? Or do you want to include our client, the little man with the palindromic first name? That seems farfetched to me, but – '

'The caterer, Chip.'

'Oh. Well, he says she was just there to do a job. No interest in books, no interest in manuscripts, no real interest in the world of mysteries. Certainly no interest in Cornell Woolrich.'

'And she stayed when her staff went home.'

'To have a drink and be sociable. He had hopes she'd spend the night, but it didn't happen. I suppose technically she's a suspect, but – '

'At the very least she's a witness,' he said. 'Bring her.'

'Bring her?'

He nodded. 'Bring them all.'

It's a shame this is a short story. If it were a novel, now would be the time for me to give you a full description of the off-street carriage house on West Twentieth Street, which Leo Haig owns and where he occupies the top two floors, having rented out the lower two stories to Madam Juana and her All-Girl Enterprise. You'd hear how Haig had lived for years in two rooms in the Bronx, breeding tropical fish and reading detective stories, until a modest inheritance allowed him to set up shop as a poor man's Nero Wolfe.

He's quirky, God knows, and I could fill a few pleasant pages recounting his quirks, including his having hired me as much for my writing ability as for my potential value as a detective. I'm expected to write up his cases the same way Archie Goodwin writes up Wolfe's, and this case was a slam-dunk, really, and he says it wouldn't stretch into a novel, but that it should work nicely as a short story.

So all I'll say is this. Haig's best quirk is his unshakable belief that Nero Wolfe exists. Under another name, of course, to protect his inviolable privacy. And the legendary brownstone, with all its different fictitious street numbers, isn't on West 35th Street at all but in another part of town entirely.

And someday, if Leo Haig performs with sufficient brilliance as a private investigator, he hopes to get the ultimate reward – an invitation to dinner at Nero Wolfe's table.

Well, that gives you an idea. If you want more in the way of background, I can only refer you to my previous writings on the subject. There have been two novels so far, *Make Out With Murder* and *The Topless Tulip Caper*, and they're full of inside stuff about Leo Haig. (There were two earlier books from before I met Haig, *No Score* and *Chip Harrison Scores Again,* but they're not mysteries and Haig's not in them. All they do, really, is tell you more than you'd probably care to know about me.)

Well, end of commercial. Haig said I should put it in, and I generally do what he tells me. After all, the man pays my salary.

And, in his own quiet way, he's a genius. As you'll see.

'They'll never come here,' I told him. 'Not today. I know it will always live in your memory as The Day the Cichlids Spawned, but to everybody else it's Christmas, and they'll want to spend it in the bosoms of their families, and – '

'Not everyone has a family,' he pointed out, 'and not every family has a bosom.'

'The Corn-Wallaces have a family. Zoltan Mihalyi

doesn't, but he's probably got somebody with a bosom lined up to spend the day with. I don't know about the others, but – '

'Bring them,' he said, 'but not here. I want them all assembled at five o'clock this afternoon at the scene of the crime.'

'The bookshop? You're willing to leave the house?'

'It's not entirely business,' he said. 'Our client is more than a client. He's a friend, and an important source of books. The reading copies he so disdains have enriched our own library immeasurably. And you know how important that is.'

If there's anything you need to know, you can find it in the pages of a detective novel. That's Haig's personal conviction, and I'm beginning to believe he's right.

'I'll pay him a visit,' he went on. 'I'll arrive at 4:30 or so, and perhaps I'll come across a book or two that I'll want for our library. You'll arrange that they all arrive around five, and we'll clear up this little business.' He frowned in thought. 'I'll tell Wong we'll want Christmas dinner at eight tonight. That should give us more than enough time.'

Again, if this were a novel, I'd spend a full chapter telling you what I went through getting them all present and accounted for. It was hard enough finding them, and then I had to sell them on coming. I pitched the event as a second stage of last night's party – their host had arranged, for their entertainment and edification, that they should be present while a real-life private detective solved an actual crime before their very eyes.

According to Haig, all we'd need to spin this yarn into a full-length book would be a dead body, although two would be better. If, say, our client had wandered into his library that morning to find a corpse seated in his favorite chair, *and* the Woolrich manuscript gone, then I could easily stretch all this to sixty thousand words. If the dead man had been wearing a deerstalker cap and holding a violin, we'd be especially well off; when the book came out, all the Sherlockian completists would be compelled to buy it.

Sorry. No murders, no Baker Street Irregulars, no dogs barking or not barking. I had to get them all there, and I did, but don't ask me how. I can't take the time to tell you.

'Now,' Zoltan Mihalyi said. 'We are all here. So can someone please tell me *why* we are all here?' There was a twinkle in his dark eyes as he spoke, and the trace of a knowing smile on his lips. He wanted an answer, but he was going to remain charming while he got it. I could believe he swept a lot of women off their feet.

'First of all,' Jeanne Botleigh said, 'I think we should

each have a glass of eggnog. It's festive, and it will help put us all in the spirit of the day.'

She was the caterer, and she was some cupcake, all right. Close-cut brown hair framed her small oval face and set off a pair of China-blue eyes. She had an English accent, roughed up some by ten years in New York, and she was short and slender and curvy, and I could see why our client had hoped she would stick around.

And now she'd whipped up a batch of eggnog, and ladled out cups for each of us. I waited until someone else tasted it – after all the mystery novels Haig's forced on me, I've developed an imagination – but once the Corn-Wallaces had tossed off theirs with no apparent effect, I took a sip. It was smooth and delicious, and it had a kick like a mule. I looked over at Haig, who's not much of a drinker, and he was smacking his lips over it.

'Why are we here?' he said, echoing the violinist's question. 'Well, sir, I shall tell you. We are here as friends and customers of our host, whom we may be able to assist in the solution of a puzzle. Last night all of us, with the exception of course of myself and my young assistant, were present in this room. Also present was the original manuscript of an unpublished novel by Cornell Woolrich. This morning we were all gone, and so was the manuscript. Now we have returned. The manuscript, alas, has not.'

'Wait a minute,' Jon Corn-Wallace said. 'You're saying one of us took it?'

'I say only that it has gone, sir. It is possible that someone within this room was involved in its disappearance, but there are diverse other possibilities as well. What impels me, what has prompted me to summon you here, is the likelihood that one or more of you knows something that will shed light on the incident.'

'But the only person who would know anything would be the person who took it,' Harriet Quinlan said. She was what they call a woman of a certain age, which generally means a woman of an uncertain age. Her figure was a few pounds beyond girlish, and I had a hunch she dyed her hair and might have had her face lifted somewhere along the way, but whatever she'd done had paid off. She was probably old enough to be my mother's older sister, but that didn't keep me from having the sort of ideas a nephew's not supposed to have.

Haig told her anyone could have observed something, and not just the guilty party, and Philip Perigord started to ask a question, and Haig held up a hand and cut him off in mid-sentence. Most people probably would have finished what they were saying, but I guess Perigord was used to studio executives shutting him up at pitch meetings. He bit off his word in the middle of a syllable and stayed mute.

'It is a holiday,' Haig said, 'and we all have other things to do, so we'd best avoid distraction. Hence I will ask the questions and you will answer them. Mr Corn-Wallace. You are a book collector. Have you given a thought to collecting manuscripts?'

'I've thought about it,' Jon Corn-Wallace said. He was the best-dressed man in the room, looking remarkably comfortable in a dark blue suit and a striped tie. He wore bull and bear cufflinks and one of those watches that's worth $5000 if it's real or $25 if you bought it from a Nigerian street vendor. 'He tried to get me interested,' he said, with a nod toward our client. 'But I was always the kind of trader who stuck to listed stocks.'

'Meaning?'

'Meaning it's impossible to pinpoint the market value of a one-of-a-kind item like a manuscript. There's too much guesswork involved. I'm not buying books with an eye to selling them, that's something my heirs will have to worry about, but I do like to know what my collection is worth and whether or not it's been a good investment. It's part of the pleasure of collecting, as far as I'm concerned. So I've stayed away from manuscripts. They're too iffy.'

'And had you had a look at *As Dark as It Gets*?'

'No. I'm not interested in manuscripts, and I don't care at all for Woolrich.'

'Jon likes hard-boiled fiction,' his wife put in, 'but

Woolrich is a little weird for his taste. I think he was a genius myself. Quirky and tormented, maybe, but what genius isn't?'

Haig, I thought. You couldn't call him tormented, but maybe he made up for it by exceeding the usual quota of quirkiness.

'Anyway,' Jayne Corn-Wallace said, 'I'm the Woolrich fan in the family. Though I agree with Jon as far as manuscripts are concerned. The value is pure speculation. And who wants to buy something and then have to get a box made for it? It's like buying an unframed canvas and having to get it framed.'

'The Woolrich manuscript was already boxed,' Haig pointed out.

'I mean generally, as an area for collecting. As a collector, I wasn't interested in *As Dark as It Gets*. If someone fixed it up and completed it, and if someone published it, I'd have been glad to buy it. I'd have bought two copies.'

'Two copies, madam?'

She nodded. 'One to read and one to own.'

Haig's face darkened, and I thought he might offer his opinion of people who were afraid to damage their books by reading them. But he kept it to himself, and I was just as glad, Jayne Corn-Wallace was a tall, handsome woman, radiating self-confidence, and I sensed she'd give as good as she got in an exchange with Haig.

'You might have wanted to read the manuscript,' Haig suggested.

She shook her head. 'I like Woolrich,' she said, 'but as a stylist he was choppy enough *after* editing and polishing. I wouldn't want to try him in manuscript, let alone an unfinished manuscript like that one.'

'Mr Mihalyi,' Haig said. 'You collect manuscripts, don't you?'

'I do.'

'And do you care for Woolrich?'

The violinist smiled. 'If I had the chance to buy the original manuscript of *The Bride Wore Black*,' he said, 'I would leap at it. If it were close at hand, and if strong drink had undermined my moral fiber, I might even slip it under my coat and walk off with it.' A wink showed us he was kidding. 'Or at least I'd have been tempted. The work in question, however, tempted me not a whit.'

'And why is that, sir?'

Mihalyi frowned. 'There are people,' he said, 'who attend open rehearsals and make surreptitious recordings of the music. They treasure them and even bootleg them to other like-minded fans. I despise such people.'

'Why?'

'They violate the artist's privacy,' he said. 'A rehearsal is a time when one refines one's approach to a piece of music. One takes chances, one uses the occasion as the equivalent of an artist's sketch pad. The person who records it is in essence spraying a rough sketch with fixative and hanging it on the wall of his personal museum. I find it unsettling enough that listeners record concert performances, making permanent what was supposed to be a transitory experience. But to record a rehearsal is an atrocity.'

'And a manuscript?'

'A manuscript is the writer's completed work. It provides a record of how he arranged and revised his ideas, and how they were in turn adjusted for better or worse by an editor. But it is finished work. An unfinished manuscript …'

'Is a rehearsal?'

'That or something worse. I ask myself, What would Woolrich have wanted?'

'Another drink,' Edward Everett Stokes said, and leaned forward to help himself to more eggnog. 'I take your point, Mihalyi. And Woolrich might well have preferred to have his unfinished work destroyed upon his death, but he left no instructions to that effect, so how can we presume to guess his wishes? Perhaps, for all we know, there is a single scene in the book that meant as much to him as anything he'd written. Or less than a scene – a bit of dialogue, a paragraph of description, perhaps no more than a single sentence. Who are we to say it should not survive?'

'Perigord,' Mihalyi said. 'You are a writer. Would you care to have your unfinished work published after your death? Would you not recoil at that, or at having it completed by others?'

Philip Perigord cocked an eyebrow. 'I'm the wrong person to ask,' he said. 'I've spent twenty years in Hollywood. Forget unfinished work. My *finished* work doesn't get published, or "produced," as they so revealingly term it. I get paid, and the work winds up on a shelf. And, when it comes to having one's work completed by others, in Hollywood you don't have to wait until you're dead. It happens during your lifetime, and you learn to live with it.'

'We don't know the author's wishes,' Harriet Quinlan put in, 'and I wonder how relevant they are.'

'But it's his work,' Mihalyi pointed out.

'Is it, Zoltan? Or does it belong to the ages? Finished or not, the author has left it to us. Schubert did not finish one of his greatest symphonies. Would you have laid its two completed movements in the casket with him?'

'It has been argued that the work was complete, that he intended it to be but two movements long.'

'That begs the question, Zoltan.'

'It does, dear lady,' he said with a wink. 'I'd rather beg the question than be undone by it. Of course I'd keep the Unfinished Symphony in the repertoire. On the other hand, I'd hate to see some fool attempt to finish it.'

'No one has, have they?'

'Not to my knowledge. But several writers have had the effrontery to finish *The Mystery of Edwin Drood*, and I do think Dickens would have been better served if the manuscript had gone in the box with his bones. And as for sequels, like those for *Pride and Prejudice* and *The Big Sleep*, or that young fellow who had the colossal gall to tread in Rex Stout's immortal footsteps ...'

Now we were getting onto sensitive ground. As far as Leo Haig was concerned, Archie Goodwin had always written up Wolfe's cases, using the transparent pseudonym of Rex Stout. (Rex Stout = fat king, an allusion to Wolfe's own regal corpulence.) Robert Goldsborough, credited with the books written since the 'death' of Stout, was, as Haig saw it, a ghostwriter employed by Goodwin, who was no longer up to the chore of hammering out the books. He'd relate them to Goldsborough, who transcribed them and polished them up. While they might not have all the narrative verve of Goodwin's own work, still they provided an important and accurate account of Wolfe's more recent cases.

See, Haig feels the great man's still alive and still raising orchids and nailing killers. Maybe somewhere on the Upper East Side. Maybe in Murray Hill, or just off Gramercy Park ...

The discussion about Goldsborough, and about sequels

in general, roused Haig from a torpor that Wolfe himself might have envied. 'Enough,' he said with authority. 'There's no time for meandering literary conversations, nor would Chip have room for them in a short-story-length report. So let us get to it. One of you took the manuscript, box and all, from its place on the shelf. Mr Mihalyi, you have the air of one who protests too much. You profess no interest in the manuscripts of unpublished novels, and I can accept that you did not yearn to possess *As Dark as It Gets,* but you wanted a look at it, didn't you?'

'I don't own a Woolrich manuscript,' he said, 'and of course I was interested in seeing what one looked like. How he typed, how he entered corrections ...'

'So you took the manuscript from the shelf.'

'Yes,' the violinist agreed. 'I went into the other room with it, opened the box and flipped through the pages. You can taste the flavor of the man's work in the visual appearance of his manuscript pages. The words and phrases x'd out, the pencil notations, the crossovers, even the typographical errors. The computer age puts paid to all that, doesn't it? Imagine Chandler running Spel-Chek, or Hammett with justified margins.' He sighed. 'A few minutes with the script made me long to own one of Woolrich's. But not this one, for reasons I've already explained.'

'You spent how long with the book?'

'Fifteen minutes at the most. Probably more like ten.'

'And returned to this room?'

'Yes.'

'And brought the manuscript with you?'

'Yes. I intended to return it to the shelf, but someone was standing in the way. It may have been you, Jon. It was someone tall, and you're the tallest person here.' He turned to our client. 'It wasn't you. But I think you may have been talking with Jon. Someone was, at any rate, and I'd have had to step between the two of you to put the box back, and that might have led to questions as to why I'd picked it up in the first place. So I put it down.'

'Where?'

'On a table. That one, I think.'

'It's not there now,' Jon Corn-Wallace said.

'It's not,' Haig agreed. 'One of you took it from that table. I could, through an exhausting process of cross-questioning, establish who that person is. But it would save us all time if the person would simply recount what happened next.'

There was a silence while they all looked at each other. 'Well, I guess this is where I come in,' Jayne Corn-Wallace said. 'I was sitting in the red chair, where Phil Perigord is sitting now. And whoever I'd been talking to went to get another drink, and I looked around, and there it was on the table.'

'The manuscript, madam?'

'Yes, but I didn't know that was what it was, not at first. I thought it was a finely bound limited edition. Because the manuscripts are all kept on that shelf, you know, and this one wasn't. And it hadn't been on the table a few minutes earlier, either. I knew that much. So I assumed it was a book someone had been leafing through, and I saw it was by Cornell Woolrich, and I didn't recognize the title, so I thought I'd try leafing through it myself.'

'And you found it was a manuscript.'

'Well, that didn't take too keen an eye, did it? I suppose I glanced at the first twenty pages, just riffled through them while the party went on around me. I stopped after a chapter or so. That was plenty.'

'You didn't like what you read?'

'There were corrections,' she said disdainfully. 'Words and whole sentences crossed out, new words penciled in. I realize writers have to work that way, but when I read a book I like to believe it emerged from the writer's mind fully formed.'

'Like Athena from the brow of What's-his-name,' her husband said.

'Zeus. I don't want to know there was a writer at work, making decisions, putting words down and then changing them. I want to forget about the writer entirely and lose myself in the story.'

'Everybody wants to forget about the writer,' Philip Perigord said, helping himself to more eggnog. 'At the Oscars each year some ninny intones, "In the beginning was the Word," before he hands out the screenwriting awards. And you hear the usual crap about how they owe it all to chaps like me who put words in their mouths. They say it, but nobody believes it. Jack Warner called us schmucks with Underwoods. Well, we've come a long way. Now we're schmucks with Power Macs.'

'Indeed,' Haig said. 'You looked at the manuscript, didn't you, Mr Perigord?'

'I never read unpublished work. Can't risk leaving myself open to a plagiarism charge.'

'Oh? But didn't you have a special interest in Woolrich? Didn't you once adapt a story of his?'

'How did you know about that? I was one of several who made a living off that particular piece of crap. It was never produced.'

'And you looked at this manuscript in the hope that you might adapt it?'

The writer shook his head. 'I'm through wasting myself out there.'

'They're through with you,' Harriet Quinlan said. 'Nothing personal, Phil, but it's a town that uses up writers and throws them away. You couldn't get arrested out there. So you've come back east to write books.'

'And you'll be representing him, madam?'

'I may, if he brings me something I can sell. I saw him paging through a manuscript and figured he was looking for something he could steal. Oh, don't look so outraged, Phil. Why not steal from Woolrich, for God's sake? He's not going to sue. He left everything to Columbia University, and you could knock off anything of his, published or unpublished, and they'd never know the difference. Ever since I saw you reading, I've been wondering. Did you come across anything worth stealing?'

'I don't steal,' Perigord said. 'Still, perfectly legitimate inspiration *can* result from a glance at another man's work –'

'I'll say it can. And did it?'

He shook his head. 'If there was a strong idea anywhere in that manuscript, I couldn't find it in the few minutes I spent looking. What about you, Harriet? I know you had a look at it, because I saw you.'

'I just wanted to see what it was you'd been so caught up in. And *I* wondered if the manuscript might be salvageable. One of my writers might be able to pull it off, and do a better job than the hack who finished *Into the Night*.'

'Ah,' Haig said. 'And what did you determine, madam?'

'I didn't read enough to form a judgment. Anyway, *Into the Night* was no great commercial success, so why tag along in its wake?'

'So you put the manuscript ...'

'Back in its box, and left it on the table where I'd found it.'

Our client shook his head in wonder. *'Murder on the Orient Express,'* he said. 'Or in the Calais coach, depending on whether you're English or American. It's beginning to look as though *everyone* read that manuscript. And I never noticed a thing!'

'Well, you were hitting the sauce pretty good,' Jon Corn-Wallace reminded him. 'And you were, uh, concentrating all your social energy in one direction.'

'How's that?'

Corn-Wallace nodded toward Jeanne Botleigh, who was refilling someone's cup. 'As far as you were concerned, our lovely caterer was the only person in the room.'

There was an awkward silence, with our host coloring and his caterer lowering her eyes demurely. Haig broke it. 'To continue,' he said abruptly. 'Miss Quinlan returned the manuscript to its box and to its place upon the table. Then –'

'But she didn't,' Perigord said. 'Harriet, I wanted another look at Woolrich. Maybe I'd missed something. But first I saw you reading it, and when I looked a second time it was gone. You weren't reading it and it wasn't on the table, either.'

'I put it back,' the agent said.

'But not where you found it,' said Edward Everett

Stokes. 'You set it down not on the table but on that revolving bookcase.'

'Did I? I suppose it's possible. But how did you know that?'

'Because I saw you,' said the small-press publisher. 'And because I wanted a look at the manuscript myself. I knew about it, including the fact that it was not restorable in the fashion of *Into the Night*. That made it valueless to a commercial publisher, but the idea of a Woolrich novel going unpublished ate away at me. I mean, we're talking about Cornell Woolrich.'

'And you thought – '

'I thought why not publish it as is, warts and all? I could do it, in an edition of two or three hundred copies, for collectors who'd happily accept inconsistencies and omissions for the sake of having something otherwise unobtainable. I wanted a few minutes' peace and quiet with the book, so I took it into the lavatory.'

'And?'

'And I read it, or at least paged through it. I must have spent half an hour in there, or close to it.'

'I remember you were gone a while,' Jon Corn-Wallace said. 'I thought you'd headed on home.'

'I thought he was in the other room,' Jayne said, 'cavorting on the pile of coats with Harriet here. But I guess that must have been someone else.'

'It was Zoltan,' the agent said, 'and we were hardly cavorting.'

'Canoodling, then, but – '

'He was teaching me a yogic breathing technique, not that it's any of your business. Stokes, you took the manuscript into the John. I trust you brought it back?'

'Well, no.'

'You took it home? You're the person responsible for its disappearance?'

'Certainly not. I didn't take it home, and I hope I'm not responsible for its disappearance. I left it in the lavatory.'

'You just left it there?'

'In its box, on the shelf over the vanity. I set it down there while I washed my hands, and I'm afraid I forgot it. And no, it's not there now. I went and looked as soon as I realized what all this was about, and I'm afraid some other hands than mine must have moved it. I'll tell you this – when it does turn up, I definitely want to publish it.'

'*If* it turns up,' our client said darkly. 'Once E. E. left it in the bathroom, anyone could have slipped it under his coat without being seen. And I'll probably never see it again.'

'But that means one of us is a thief,' somebody said.

'I know, and that's out of the question. You're all my friends. But we were all drinking last night, and drink can confuse a person. Suppose one of you did take it from the

211

bathroom and carried it home as a joke, the kind of joke that can seem funny after a few drinks. If you could contrive to return it, perhaps in such a way that no one could know your identity ... Haig, you ought to be able to work that out.'

'I could,' Haig agreed. 'If that were how it happened. But it didn't.'

'It didn't?'

'You forget the least obvious suspect.'

'Me? Dammit, Haig, are you saying I stole my own manuscript?'

'I'm saying the butler did it,' Haig said, 'or the closest thing we have to a butler. Miss Botleigh, your upper lip has been trembling almost since we all sat down. You've been on the point of an admission throughout and haven't said a word. Have you in fact read the manuscript of *As Dark as It Gets*?'

'Yes.'

The client gasped. 'You have? When?'

'Last night.'

'But – '

'I had to use the lavatory,' she said, 'and the book was there, although I could see it wasn't an ordinary bound book but pages in a box. I didn't think I would hurt it by looking at it. So I sat there and read the first two chapters.'

'What did you think?' Haig asked her.

'It was very powerful. Parts of it were hard to follow, but the scenes were strong, and I got caught up in them.'

'That's Woolrich,' Jayne Corn-Wallace said. 'He can grab you, all right.'

'And then you took it with you when you went home,' our client said. 'You were so involved you couldn't bear to leave it unfinished, so you, uh, borrowed it.' He reached to pat her hand. 'Perfectly understandable,' he said, 'and perfectly innocent. You were going to bring it back once you'd finished it. So all this fuss has been over nothing.'

'That's not what happened.'

'It's not?'

'I read two chapters,' she said, 'and I thought I'd ask to borrow it some other time, or maybe not. But I put the pages back in the box and left them there.'

'In the bathroom?'

'Yes.'

'So you never did finish the book,' our client said. 'Well, if it ever turns up I'll be more than happy to lend it to you, but until then – '

'But perhaps Miss Botleigh has already finished the book,' Haig suggested.

'How could she? She just told you she left it in the bathroom.'

Haig said, 'Miss Botleigh?'

LAWRENCE BLOCK

'I finished the book,' she said. 'When everybody else went home, I stayed.'

'My word,' Zoltan Mihalyi said. 'Woolrich never had a more devoted fan, or one half so beautiful.'

'Not to finish the manuscript,' she said, and turned to our host. 'You asked me to stay,' she said.

'I *wanted* you to stay,' he agreed. 'I wanted to *ask* you to stay. But I don't remember ...'

'I guess you'd had quite a bit to drink,' she said, 'although you didn't show it. But you asked me to stay, and I'd been hoping you would ask me, because I wanted to stay.'

'You must have had rather a lot to drink yourself,' Harriet Quinlan murmured.

'Not that much,' said the caterer. 'I wanted to stay because he's a very attractive man.'

Our client positively glowed, then turned red with embarrassment. 'I knew I had a hole in my memory,' he said, 'but I didn't think anything significant could have fallen through it. So you actually stayed? God. What, uh, happened?'

'We went upstairs,' Jeanne Botleigh said. 'And we went to the bedroom, and we went to bed.'

'Indeed,' said Haig.

'And it was ...'

'Quite wonderful,' she said.

'And I don't remember. I think I'm going to kill myself.'

'Not on Christmas Day,' E. E. Stokes said. 'And not with a mystery still unsolved. Haig, what became of the bloody manuscript?'

'Miss Botleigh?'

She looked at our host, then lowered her eyes. 'You went to sleep afterward,' she said, 'and I felt entirely energized, and knew I couldn't sleep, and I thought I'd read for a while. And I remembered the manuscript, so I came down here and fetched it.'

'And read it?'

'In bed. I thought you might wake up, in fact I was hoping you would. But you didn't.'

'Damn it,' our client said, with feeling.

'So I finished the manuscript and still didn't feel sleepy. And I got dressed and let myself out and went home.'

There was a silence, broken at length by Zoltan Mihalyi, offering our client congratulations on his triumph and sympathy for the memory loss. 'When you write your memoirs,' he said, 'you'll have to leave that chapter blank.'

'Or have someone ghost it for you,' Philip Perigord offered.

'The manuscript,' Stokes said. 'What became of it?'

'I don't know,' the caterer said. 'I finished it –'

'Which is more than Woolrich could say,' Jayne Corn-Wallace said.

' – and I left it there.'

'There?'

'In its box. On the bedside table, where you'd be sure to find it first thing in the morning. But I guess you didn't.'

'The manuscript? Haig, you're telling me you want the *manuscript!*'

'You find my fee excessive?'

'But it wasn't even lost. No one took it. It was next to my bed. I'd have found it sooner or later.'

'But you didn't,' Haig said. 'Not until you'd cost me and my young associate the better part of our holiday. You've been reading mysteries all your life. Now you got to see one solved in front of you, and in your own magnificent library.'

He brightened. 'It is a nice room, isn't it?'

'It's first-rate.'

'Thanks. But Haig, listen to reason. You did solve the puzzle and recover the manuscript, but now you're demanding what you recovered as compensation. That's like rescuing a kidnap victim and insisting on adopting the child yourself.'

'Nonsense. It's nothing like that.'

'All right, then it's like recovering stolen jewels and demanding the jewels themselves as reward. It's just plain disproportionate. I hired you because I wanted the manuscript in my collection, and now you expect to wind up with it in *your* collection.'

It did sound a little weird to me, but I kept my mouth shut. Haig had the ball, and I wanted to see where he'd go with it.

He put his fingertips together. 'In *Black Orchids,*' he said, 'Wolfe's client was his friend Lewis Hewitt. As recompense for his work, Wolfe insisted on all of the black orchid plants Hewitt had bred. Not one. All of them.'

'That always seemed greedy to me.'

'If we were speaking of fish,' Haig went on, 'I might be similarly inclined. But books are of use to me only as reading material. I want to *read* that book, sir, and I want to have it close to hand if I need to refer to it.' He shrugged. 'But I don't need the original that you prize so highly. Make me a copy.'

'A copy?'

'Indeed. Have the manuscript photocopied.'

'You'd be content with a ... a copy?'

'And a credit,' I said quickly, before Haig could give away the store. We'd put in a full day, and he ought to get more than a few hours' reading out of it. 'A two thousand dollar store credit,' I added, 'which Mr Haig can use up as he sees fit.'

'Buying paperbacks and book-club editions,' our client

said. 'It should last you for years.' He heaved a sigh. 'A photocopy and a store credit. Well, if that makes you happy ...'

And that pretty much wrapped it up. I ran straight home and sat down at the typewriter, and if the story seems a little hurried it's because I was in a rush when I wrote it. See, our client tried for a second date with Jeanne Botleigh, to refresh his memory, I suppose, but a woman tends to feel less than flattered when you forget having gone to bed with her, and she wasn't having any.

So I called her the minute I got home, and we talked about this and that, and we've got a date in an hour and a half. I'll tell you this much, if I get lucky, I'll remember. So wish me luck, huh?

And, by the way ...

Merry Christmas!

On Christmas Day
in the Morning

Margery Allingham

Sir Leo Pursuivant, the Chief Constable, had been sitting
in his comfortable study after a magnificent lunch and
talking heavily of the sadness of Christmas, while his
guest, Mr Campion, most favoured of his large house-
party, had been laughing at him gently.

It was true, the younger man had admitted, his pale eyes
sleepy behind his horn-rimmed spectacles, that, however
good the organization, the festival was never quite the
same after one was six and a half, but then, what sensible
man would expect it to be, and meanwhile, what a truly
remarkable bird that had been!

At that point the Superintendent had arrived with

his grim little story and the atmosphere was spoiled altogether.

The policeman sat in a highbacked chair, against a panelled wall festooned with holly and tinsel, his round black eyes hard and preoccupied under his short grey hair. Superintendent Pussey was one of those lean and urgent countrymen who never quite lose their innate fondness for a wonder. Despite years of experience the thing that simply could not have happened and yet indubitably *had* retained a place in his cosmos. He was holding forth about the latest example. It had already ruined his Christmas and had kept a great many other people out in the sleet all day, but nothing would induce him to leave it alone even for five minutes. A heap of turkey sandwiches was disappearing as he talked and a glass of scotch and soda stood untasted at his side.

'You can see I had to come at once,' he was saying. 'I had to. I don't see what happened and that's a fact. It's a sort of miracle. Besides, fancy killing a poor old postman on Christmas morning! That's inhuman isn't it? Unnatural?'

Sir Leo nodded his white head. 'Let me get this clear: the dead man appears to have been run down at the Benham cross roads ...'

Pussey took a handful of cigarettes from the box at his side and arranged them in a cross on the shining surface of the table.

'Look,' he said, 'here is the Ashby road with a slight bend in it and here, running at right angles, slap through the curve, is the Benham road. You know as well as I do, sir, they're both good wide main thoroughfares as roads go in these parts. This morning the Benham postman, old Fred Noakes, came along the Benham Road loaded down with mail.'

'On a bicycle,' murmured Campion.

'Naturally. On a bicycle. He called at the last farm before the cross roads and left just about ten o' clock. We know that because he had a cup of tea there. Then his way led him over the crossing and on towards Benham proper.'

He paused and looked up from his cigarettes.

'There was very little traffic early today, terrible weather all the time, and quite a bit of activity later, so we've got no skid marks to help us. Well, no one seems to have seen old Noakes until close on half an hour later. Then the Benham constable, who lives some three hundred yards from the crossing, came out of his house and walked down to his gate. He saw the postman at once, lying in the middle of the road across his machine. He was dead then.'

'He had been trying to carry on?'

'Yes. He was walking, pushing the bike, and he'd dropped in his tracks. There was a depressed fracture in the side of his skull where something – say a car mirror – had struck him. I've got the doctor's report. Meanwhile there's something else.'

He returned to his second line of cigarettes.

'Just about ten o'clock there were a couple of fellows walking here on the *Ashby* road. They report that they were almost run down by a saloon car which came up behind them. It missed them and careered off out of their sight round the bend towards the crossing.

'A few minutes later, half a mile farther on, on the other side of the cross roads, a police car met and succeeded in stopping, the same saloon. There was a row and the driver, getting the wind up suddenly, started up again, skidded and smashed the vehicle on the nearest telephone pole. The car turned out to be stolen and there were four half full bottles of gin in the back. The two occupants were both fighting drunk and are now detained.'

Mr Campion took off his spectacles and blinked at the speaker.

'You suggest that there was a connection, do you? Fred and the gin drinkers met at the cross roads, in fact. Any signs on the car?'

Pussey shrugged his shoulders. 'Our chaps are at work on that now. The second smash has complicated things a bit but last time I 'phoned they were hopeful.'

'But my dear fellow!' Sir Leo was puzzled. 'If you can

get expert evidence of a collision between the car and the postman, your worries are over. That is, of course, if the medical evidence permits the theory that the unfortunate fellow picked himself up and struggled the three hundred yards towards the constable's house.'

Pussey hesitated.

'There's the trouble,' he admitted. 'If that was all we'd be sitting pretty, but it's not and I'll tell you why. In that three hundred yards of Benham Road, between the crossing and the spot where old Fred died, there is a stile which leads to a footpath. Down the footpath, the best part of a quarter of a mile away, there is one small cottage and at that cottage letters were delivered this morning. The doctor says Noakes might have staggered the three hundred yards up the road leaning on his bike but he puts his foot down and says the other journey, over the stile, would have been plain impossible. I've talked to him. He's the best man in the world on the job and we shan't shake him on that.'

'All of which would argue,' observed Mr Campion brightly, 'that the postman met the car after he came back from the cottage – between the stile and the policeman's house.'

'That's what the constable thought.' Pussey's black eyes were snapping. 'As soon as he'd telephoned for help he slipped down to the cottage to see if Noakes had called there. When he found he had, he searched the road. He was mystified though because both he and his missus had been at their window for an hour watching for the mail and they hadn't seen a vehicle of any sort go by either way. If a car did hit the postman where he fell it must have turned and gone back afterwards and that's impossible, for the patrol would have seen it.'

Leo frowned at him. 'What about the other witnesses? Did they see any second car?'

'No.' Pussey's face shone with honest wonder. 'I made sure of that. Everybody sticks to it that there was no other car or cart about and a good job too, they say, considering the way the saloon was being driven. As I see it, it's a proper mystery, a kind of not very nice miracle, and those two beauties are going to get away with murder on the strength of it. Whatever our fellows find on the car they'll never get past the doctor's evidence.'

Mr Campion got up sadly. The sleet was beating on the windows and from inside the house came the more cheerful sound of teacups. He nodded to the Chief Constable.

'I fear we shall have to see that footpath before it gets utterly dark, you know,' he said. 'In this weather conditions may have changed by tomorrow.'

Leo sighed.

They stopped their freezing journey at the Benham police station to pick up the constable, who proved to be a pleasant youngster who had known and liked the postman and was anxious to serve as their guide.

They inspected the cross roads and the bend and the spot where the saloon had come to grief. By the time they reached the stile the world was grey and dismal and all trace of Christmas had vanished.

Mr Campion climbed over and the others followed him on to the path which was narrow and slippery. It wound out into the mist before them, apparently without end.

The procession slid and scrambled in silence for what seemed a mile only to encounter yet another stile and a plank bridge over a stream leading to a patch of bog. As he struggled out of it Pussey pushed back his dripping hat and gazed at the constable.

'You're not having a game I suppose?' he enquired briefly.

'No, sir, no. The little house is just here. You can't make it out because it's a little bit low. There it is, sir.'

He pointed to a hump in the near distance which they had all taken to be a haystack and which now emerged as the roof of a hovel with its back towards them in the wet waste.

'Good Heavens!' Leo regarded its desolation with dismay. 'Does anybody actually live here?'

'Oh yes, sir. An old widow lady. Mrs Fyson's the name.'

'Alone? How old?'

'I don't rightly know, sir. Over seventy five, must be.'

Leo grunted and a silence fell on the company. The scene was so forlorn and so unutterably quiet in its loneliness that the world might have died.

Mr Campion broke the spell.

'This is definitely no walk for a dying man,' he said firmly. 'The doctor's evidence is completely convincing, don't you think? Now we're here perhaps we should drop in and see the householder.'

'We can't all *get* in,' Leo objected. 'Perhaps the Superintendent ...?'

'No. You and I will go.' Mr Campion was obstinate, and taking the Chief Constable's arm led him firmly round to the front of the cottage. There was a yellow light in the single window on the ground floor and as they slid up a narrow brick path to a very small door, Leo hung back.

'I hate this,' he muttered. 'Oh – all right, go on. Knock if you must.'

Mr Campion obeyed, stooping so that his head might miss the lintel. There was a movement inside and, at once, the door was opened very wide so that he was startled by the rush of warmth from within.

A little old woman stood before him, peering up without astonishment. He was principally aware of bright eyes.

'Oh dear,' she said unexpectedly. 'You *are* damp. Come

in.' And then, looking past him at the skulking Leo. 'Two of you! Well, isn't that nice. Mind your poor heads.'

The visit became a social occasion before they were well in the room. Her complete lack of surprise or question coupled with the extreme lowness of the ceiling gave her an advantage from which the interview never entirely recovered.

From the first she did her best to put them at their ease.

'You'll have to sit down at once,' she said, waving them to two chairs, one on either side of the small black kitchener. 'Most people have to. I'm all right, you see, because I'm not tall. This is my chair here. You must undo that,' she went on touching Leo's coat, 'otherwise you may take cold when you go out. It is so very chilly isn't it? But so seasonable and that's always nice.'

Afterwards it was Mr Campion's belief that neither he nor the Chief Constable had a word to say for themselves for the first five minutes.

They were certainly seated and looking round the one downstair room the house contained before anything approaching conversation took place.

It was not a sordid interior yet the walls were discoloured, the furniture old without being in any way antique and the place could hardly have been called neat. But at the moment it was festive. There was holly over the two pictures and on the mantel, above the stove, a crowd of bright Christmas cards.

Their hostess sat between them, near the table. It was set for a small tea party and the oil lamp with the red and white frosted glass shade which stood in the centre of it shed a comfortable light on her serene face.

She was a short plump old person whose white hair was brushed tightly to her little round head. Her clothes were all knitted and of an assortment of colours and with them she wore, most unsuitably, a Maltese silk lace collarette and a heavy gold chain. It was only when they noticed she was blushing that they realized she was shy.

'Oh,' she exclaimed at last, making a move which put their dumbness to shame. 'I quite forgot to say it before! A Merry Christmas to you. Isn't it wonderful how it keeps coming round? It's such a *happy* time, isn't it?'

Leo took himself in hand.

'I do apologize,' he began. 'This is an imposition on such a day.'

'Not at all,' she said. 'Visitors are a great treat. Not everybody braves my footpath in the winter.'

'But some people do, of course?' ventured Mr Campion.

'Of course.' She shot him her shy smile. 'Always once a week. They send down from the village every Friday and only this morning a young man, the policeman to be exact, came all the way over the fields to wish me the compliments of the season and to know if I'd got my post!'

'And you had!' Leo glanced at the array of cards with relief. He was a kindly, sentimental, family man with a horror of loneliness.

She nodded at the brave collection with deep affection.

'It's lovely to see them all up there again, it's one of the real joys of Christmas, isn't it? Messages from people you love and who love you and all so *pretty*, too.'

'Did you come down bright and early to meet the postman?' The Chief Constable's question was disarmingly innocent but she looked ashamed and dropped her eyes.

'I wasn't up! Wasn't it dreadful? I was late this morning. In fact, I was only just picking the letters off the mat there when the policeman called. He helped me gather them, the nice boy. There were such a lot. I lay lazily in bed this morning thinking of them instead of moving.'

'Still, you knew they were there.'

'Oh yes.' She sounded content. 'I knew they were there. May I offer you a cup of tea? I'm waiting for my Christmas party to arrive, just a woman and her dear greedy little boy; they won't be long. In fact, when I heard your knock I thought they were here already.'

Mr Campion, who had risen to inspect the display of cards on the mantel shelf more closely, helped her to move the kettle so that it should not boil too soon.

The cards were splendid. There were nearly thirty of them in all, and the envelopes which had contained them were packed in a neat bundle and tucked behind the clock.

In design they were mostly conventional. There were robins and firesides, saints and angels, with a secondary line in pictures of gardens in unseasonable bloom, and Scots terriers in tam o' shanter caps. One magnificent affair was entirely in ivorine with a cut-out disclosing a coach and horses surrounded with roses and forget-me-nots. The written messages were all warm and personal – all breathing affection and friendliness and the outspoken joy of the season:

'The very best to you Darling from All at the Limes'; 'To dear Auntie from Little Phil'; 'Love and Memories. Edith and Ted'; 'There is no wish like the old wish. Warm regards George'; 'For dearest Mother'; 'Cheerio. Lots of love. Just off. Writing. Take care of yourself. Sonny'; 'For dear little Agnes with love from US ALL'.

Mr Campion stood before them for a long time but at length he turned away. He had to stoop to avoid the beam and yet he towered over the old woman who stood watching him.

Something had happened. It had suddenly become very still in the house. The gentle hissing of the kettle sounded unnaturally loud. The recollection of their loneliness returned to chill the cosy room.

The old lady had lost her smile and there was wariness in her eyes.

'Tell me,' Mr Campion spoke very gently. 'How do you do it? Do you put them all down there on the mat in their envelopes before you go to bed on Christmas Eve?'

While the point of his question was dawning upon Leo, there was complete silence. It was breathless and unbearable until old Mrs Fyson pierced it with a laugh of genuine naughtiness.

'Well,' she said devastatingly, 'It does make it more fun, doesn't it?' She glanced back at Leo whose handsome face was growing scarlet.

'Then ...' He was having difficulty with his voice.

'Then the postman did *not* call this morning, ma'am?'

'The postman never calls here except when he brings something from the Government,' she said pleasantly. 'Everybody gets letters from the Government nowadays, don't they? But he doesn't call here with *personal* letters because, you see, I'm the last of us.' She paused and frowned very faintly. It rippled like a shadow over the smoothness of her quiet, careless brow. 'There's been so many wars,' she said.

'But, dear Lady ...' Leo was completely overcome.

She patted his arm to comfort him.

'My dear man,' she said kindly. 'Don't be distressed. This isn't sad. It's Christmas. They sent me their love at

Christmas and *I've still got it*. At Christmas I remember them and they remember me I expect – wherever they are.' Her eyes strayed to the ivorine card with the coach on it. 'I do sometimes wonder about poor *George,*' she remarked seriously. 'He was my husband's elder brother and he really did have quite a shocking life. But he sent me that remarkable card one year and I kept it with the others … after all, we ought to be charitable, oughtn't we? At Christmas.'

As the four men plodded back through the fields, Pussey was jubilant.

'That's done the trick,' he said. 'Cleared up the mystery and made it all plain sailing. We'll get those two crooks for doing in poor old Noakes. The old girl was just cheering herself up and you fell for it, eh, constable? Oh, don't worry, my boy. There's no harm done and it's a thing that might have deceived anybody. Just let it be a lesson to you. I know how it happened. You didn't want to worry the old thing with the tale of a death on Christmas morning so you took the sight of the letters as evidence and didn't go into it. As it turned out, you were wrong. That's life.'

He thrust the young man on ahead of him and waited for Campion.

'What beats me is how you cottoned to it,' he confided. 'What gave you the idea?'

'I merely read it, I'm afraid,' Mr Campion was apologetic. 'All the envelopes were there, sticking out from behind the clock. The top one had a ha'penny stamp on it so I looked at the postmark. It was 1914.'

Pussey laughed. 'Given to you!' he chuckled. 'Still I bet you had a job to trust your own eyes.'

'Ah.' Mr Campion's voice was thoughtful in the dusk. 'That, Super, that was the really difficult bit.'

Credits